PRAISE FOR

The ending is not only satisfying, it is inspiring!
  - B.J. Bassett, author of *Lily*.

The story is gripping and moves at a satisfying pace, neither too fast nor too slow.
  -Brian Michaud, FIVE STARS

Escape to Molokai by Spike Brown is a real find.
  -Gareth Griffith, FIVE STARS

ESCAPE TO MOLOKAI

SPIKE BROWN

CHAPMAN BROWN BOOKS

ESCAPE TO MOLOKAI is a work of fiction. Names, characters, places, and incidents either are the product of the author's imagination or are used fictitiously. Any resemblance to actual persons, living or dead, events or locales is entirely coincidental.

ISBN-10: 1478384336
ISBN-13: 978-1478384335

Published by Chapman Brown Books
Copyright © 2012 Spike Brown
All rights reserved.

For my dad who loved history and
for those banished to Kalaupapa

1

NIGHT

Maui, 1946

George lit a candle on his bedside table and examined his thigh in the dim flickering light. The burn was the size of a fried egg and felt like it still smoldered. He frowned. Sometimes it felt like everything he did backfired.

Pulling a torn shred of aloe from his pocket, he squeezed the tuberous leaf until its juice dripped onto the burn. It stung and soothed at the same time. One thing for sure, he wouldn't pretend to be a fire-dancer again anytime soon. He didn't like looking stupid, not even in front of his best friend.

He smiled. Jonathan had looked pretty stupid tiptoeing across the neighbor's yard for the aloe. When Mr. Kim drove up, Jonathan had bolted like he was being chased by zombies.

Still grinning, George squeezed the leaf one last time and covered the burn with a bandage he'd filched from his grandmother's medicine cabinet. The last thing he needed was for it to get infected. Then he'd have to tell his grandmother, and he was already in enough trouble for one day.

Footsteps. He blew out the candle, stripped off his shirt, and leaped into bed—sandy shorts, dirty feet and all.

"You still awake?" Tutu came in carrying a kerosene lamp. Like always, she flipped the quilt back before sitting on the edge of the bed. George smiled. Tutu was superstitious and believed it was bad luck to sit on a quilt. She bumped up against his burned leg.

He gulped in a breath and forced a smile.

"You okay?"

"I'm fine."

She pulled a white envelope from her pocket. It had a clipped corner. "You look a little tired. It's just as well Jonathan went home. The two of you would have been up all night."

To change the subject, he pointed to the envelope. "That from my parents?"

She nodded and handed him the letter.

"Why does Dad always cut off the corner of the envelopes?" he asked.

"I don't know."

He tore it open and read. It didn't say much. Their garden was doing good. His father had fixed a leak in their roof. It ended with they missed him.

His eyes went to the framed picture of his parents on the wall. If it weren't for the picture, he'd have forgotten what they looked like. Over one corner hung a necklace with a carved bone turtle. It had been his father's. Now it was his. He never wore it, because he was afraid he might lose it.

"Tell me again why we live here on Maui and they live on Molokai," he said, even though he knew the story.

Smile lines appeared around her eyes. "Again?"

"Please?" He liked hearing the story because while she told it, he could believe it. Believe that he belonged and that his parents hadn't dumped him like a piece of unwanted trash on his grandparents' doorstep. Believe they missed him. Believe that it was the war's fault his family was scattered between the islands.

Her face softened. "Okay. Before you were born the whole family lived on the Big Island. We had a huge farm with chickens and..."

George relaxed and for a while forgot about the throbbing pain on his thigh.

". . . Times got hard and in the end we were forced to move on. Kapuna found work here on Maui at the docks. The only work your father could find was on Molokai, in the sugarcane."

Maybe it was the burn. Maybe it was something else, but he'd finally worked up the courage to ask the question he'd never dared to ask. "Why didn't he get a job here? There are sugarcane fields on Maui."

She paused for a moment. Her eyes wouldn't meet his.

"There weren't any jobs at the time," she said and patted his leg.

George winced as pain shot like lighting bolts from the burn. He grabbed her hand.

She smiled. "You and your sister were born on Molokai and—"

"And now I live here with you and Kapuna?" he finished for her.

She held him in a tight hug. "Like the sweet-scented blooms of a plumeria tree, you are my blossom of joy."

Even though he'd never admit it to anyone, especially not to Jonathan, he liked being the sweet scent of a flower to his grand-mother, and he liked being held.

Tutu tucked the quilt over his shoulders. "You sure are full of questions tonight."

"It's just that I can't remember them."

Tutu picked up the lamp and moved to the door.

"Why can't we visit them? Or they visit us?" he asked for what must have been the ten thousandth time.

"You know we can't afford to travel."

She blew out the lamp. Shadows filled the room, streaked with silver moonlight. She turned her back to him.

"What about my sister and my other grandparents? Can we visit them?"

"No." Tutu paused. "I've been meaning to tell you, Launi's moved to Molokai to live with your parents."

George sat up, his stomach suddenly queasy. His parents wanted her, but not him. "Launi gets to live with them and I don't?"

She turned, and he thought he saw tears in her eyes, but he couldn't really tell in the poor light.

When she spoke, her voice was strained. "No more questions tonight. They love you more than you'll ever know. Now go to sleep."

"Did you see the little ring around the moon?" George asked, not ready for her to leave. Not before he'd made amends for sounding ungrateful.

"Yes. Tomorrow will be a good fishing day. Kapuna and I need to be up before the sun rises."

"That's right," Kapuna said from the doorway. "Time to pack it in for the night. Tomorrow will be a busy day."

He came in as Tutu left.

"Can't I go fishing with you?" George asked. "Please?"

"Not this time. Remember, you're helping Mr. Kim in his garden."

"He always blames things on me. Even when I don't do anything."

"Mr. Kim is our neighbor and we have to get along." Kapuna ruffled George's hair. "Sometimes he is a grouch, but this time it's different. You and Jonathan pretty much trampled his garden. You'll have to undo the damage you did."

"But it was his Poi Dog's fault. He was chasing our chickens."

Kapuna sighed. "We've already been over this. You're thirteen. It's time you take on a little responsibility."

"I hate living here," George blurted. "I can't wait for my parents to send for me."

Kapuna froze. The look on his face made George regret his words for the second time that night. Why had he said that? He wished he could take back the words, but it was too late.

Kapuna tucked in the covers. "*Moi, Moi.* Sleep well, my grandson."

"I'm sorry. I didn't mean it."

"I know you didn't." Kapuna closed the bedroom door.

Stupid. Stupid. Stupid. Why had he said that to Kapuna? He didn't hate living here. He didn't want to move. This was his home. Kapuna and Tutu were his family. He just wished his parents would move to Maui and they all could live together like before the war.

What he did hate, was having to spend a whole day with Mr. Kim. The old man was never satisfied. Before tomorrow was over, he knew he'd be in some sort of new trouble—real or imagined.

Outside his window, the shadow of a palm swayed in the moonlight. It looked spooky and even a little bit mysterious. He grinned. It was perfect, because he and Jonathan had mysterious plans for the night.

A clandestine meeting at midnight!

2

FULL MOON

George waited until the house was silent. He slipped out of bed, cracked open his bedroom door, and listened. The steady rhythm of Kapuna's deep snores from the other bedroom warned intruders the house was occupied.

He crept into the kitchen to peek at the clock. It was eleven. Even though it was normally only a twenty-minute walk to the square, he decided it was time to go. The burn would slow him, and he didn't want to be late. The ritual had to take place at midnight under a full moon. If they missed it, they'd have to wait until next month, and that would be a lifetime away.

Plus, Jonathan would be mad at him if he had to wait.

George slipped out the back door. Sweet flowery scents floated on the night breeze. Walking the road would take less time, but there was a greater chance of being spotted, so he headed for the beach. He walked down the low lava rock wall that separated his yard from Mr. Kim's.

Barking erupted from the neighbor's house. It was Poi Dog. George jumped onto the grass and sprinted under a row of palm trees. The last thing he needed was for Mr. Kim to catch him in his backyard again.

He raced down the beach, past an outrigger canoe pulled high up on the sand. The burn on his leg began to throb again, and he slowed to a walk.

Thirty minutes later he neared the town square with the giant banyan tree that covered almost the whole block. He whistled to let Jonathan know he'd arrived.

Jonathan emerged from the shadows. "You're almost late," he said in a low whisper and then laughed like Bela Lugosi.

"There's plenty of time."

"You bring the knife?"

"No, I forgot."

"Then what are we going to use?"

George bent down and picked up a piece of sharp coral. "This will work. We only need a little blood."

"Okay then," Jonathan said. "Let's do it."

George stabbed his thumb. A tiny blob of blood welled on his skin. He handed the coral to Jonathan. "Your turn."

Jonathan jabbed his thumb and raised his arm. Blood trickled down his hand and into the cuff of his shirt.

"Weird," George said. "Your blood looks black in the moonlight."

"Woooo. . . that's because I'm the zombie king. Press your thumb against mine and we'll be zombie kings together."

George put his bloody thumb on Jonathan's and felt a foreboding shiver run down his arm. When he spoke, his voice came out in a loud, hoarse whisper. "Under this sacred tree, witnessed by a full moon, we make this pact."

"Forever we share the same blood."

"Together we'll stand against mummies, monsters, and denizens of the dark."

"We'll share in the fight against all curses, real and imagined."

"Blood brothers forever," George said.

"Blood brothers forever," Jonathan echoed.

"It is done," George said. "Hey, you're getting blood on your shirt."

"Shoot! My auntie will kill me." Jonathan slipped off his shirt. On his arm, a big irregular patch of white skin gleamed in the moonlight.

"Hey, your white blob has grown. It's bigger. Now it kind of looks like a ghost. Keeps growing and you'll turn into one. Does it hurt?"

"No. Not even if I scratch it." Jonathan dug his thumbnail into the white skin. "I can't feel a thing. Auntie Mary thinks it's from the sun."

"You're kidding."

"I wish I were. Then I wouldn't have to wear long-sleeved shirts all the time."

"Bummer," George said, thinking sometimes it was good to be poor. His grandparents couldn't afford dress shirts for everyday wear. He bumped his burn and winced. "Wish this burn didn't hurt."

"Your wish is my command, oh blood brother of mine. Follow me," Jonathan said and started off at a fast pace.

"Where are we going?"

Jonathan grinned. "To the Hauola seat."

George snorted. "You're crazy." A lot of stuff Jonathan believed wasn't true. The power of the Hauola seat was one of them. "It's just old superstition."

"You shouldn't make fun of what you don't understand," Jonathan said and walked faster. George had to hurry to catch up.

"Don't be mad."

"I'm not. I'm just tired of you thinking you know everything. I thought once we were blood brothers, things would change."

"Change?"

"Yeah, like you would stop making fun of the things I believe in."

"I'm not making fun of anything."

"Then you'll sit in the Hauola seat?"

"I'm following you, aren't I?"

Jonathan didn't answer.

George shoved him. "Loosen up. I can't wait to try it."

They hurried past the library to the low rock wall that bordered the bay. Moonlight glinted off the water, and it felt like they were in a black-and-white movie.

"There it is," George said, trying to sound excited, hoping to put Jonathan back into a better mood. He pointed into the water at the cluster of large rocks that circled the Hauola stone where the gods had placed the healing seat.

They moved down the wall to where it was the closest to the stone.

"You coming in?" he asked as he stripped off his pants and T-shirt.

Jonathan shook his head. "Nope. Nothing wrong with me."

"Okay." He slipped into the ocean, wearing just his underwear and the bandage on his leg. The salt water seeped through the gauze and stung his burn. He gritted his teeth.

Carefully he made his way to the Hauola stone, climbed onto its natural seat and settled his feet into a hollow footrest. He slid back a bit and leaned against the tiny lip of a backrest. It was kind of comfortable.

"What now?" he asked.

"For starters, you can laugh at my jokes," Jonathan said.

"Only if they're funny."

Carefully George peeled off the bandage and let the gentle waves lap against the wound. At first, the salt water stung like the devil, and then nothing.

"Here's one I made up myself." Jonathan cleared his throat. "In Hollywood they're calling *slippahs*, flip flops." He paused. "You're supposed to ask me why."

"Okay. Why?"

"Because if you try to flip in them, you'll flop." He waited. "You're not laughing."

George raised his leg from the water and squinted. The burn had faded to a pale white. He grinned and started laughing loud enough to be heard all the way to the mainland.

"It wasn't that funny."

George splashed his way back to shore. Jumping out, he shouted, "Look at my leg! It's healed."

Except for the loss of pigment, the skin looked almost normal.

"You're the best blood-brother ever," George said and slapped Jonathan on the back. Then he slipped into his clothes. "This calls for a celebration."

"Like what?"

"Let's have a shaved ice."

"Where?"

"At *The Dolphin* on Front Street."

"They're not open."

"So we'll help ourselves tonight and you'll pay them tomorrow."

"I don't know . . ."

A police siren pierced the silence. Its whine grew louder. In seconds, flashing red lights and bright headlights raced toward where they stood.

"Come on," George said and pulled his friend into the shadows. To his relief, the cars sped past without slowing. Two police cars followed by a black sedan. "Hey. They're turning onto your street."

"I bet it's the neighbors," Jonathan said. "They're always causing problems. Let's go spy out what's happening."

They ran down the street, keeping to the shadows. When they arrived, the cars weren't in front of the neighbor's house. They were parked in front of Jonathan's. The three cars created a barricade across the front of the yard. Two police cars and the large black sedan with the round Hawaiian Health Department seal painted on its door.

Electric lights glared from every room of the two-story house.

The front door flew open. Two police officers, a man in a black suit and a woman in a nurse's uniform led out Jonathan's cousin Alice. She was crying.

Jonathan's auntie Mary emerged, her face stricken white. She grabbed at the suited man's arm.

"Stand back," the man ordered and brushed her hand away. "Or you'll be arrested for interfering with official business."

"Wait here," Jonathan whispered. "I'll go see what's going on."

"I'm coming, too."

"There's no point in us both getting in trouble for sneaking out."

It didn't feel right, but George said, "Okay."

Jonathan stepped into the light.

"There he is!" shouted one of the officers.

Two gloved men rushed toward Jonathan and grabbed him.

Jonathan whistled three quick chirps. George knew it was a warning for him to stay hidden, but it seemed wrong. He should do something. He should help.

The tall man in the dark suit herded Jonathan and Alice into the back seat of the black car—like they were like criminals.

"Don't take them away," Auntie Mary pleaded. "They're fine. There's nothing wrong with either of them."

They were fine? What was she talking about? Of course they were fine. What was going on?

Jonathan straightened. "Don't worry, Auntie. It's a case of mistaken identity, like in the movies. Alice and I will be home tomorrow."

George knew he should do something, but what? He couldn't think.

The car engines hummed to life. The black sedan pulled away from the curb. The police cars followed.

George sunk lower into the shadows, tasting bitter bile. He'd just failed his best friend. His blood brother. The worse part was that he knew now that Jonathan had been taken, his friend wasn't going to be fine and there was nothing he could do about it.

The lights of the cars disappeared around a corner, the sound of their engines growing fainter as they drove into the night.

George was left standing alone in the dark. Alone and wondering what to do next.

3

BAD NEWS

George waited in the dark until the crickets resumed their Morse code chirps. He couldn't leave until he found out what had happened. Why the police had arrested Jonathan and Alice.

One by one, the lights went off in the house until only the faint glow of the kitchen lamp was visible.

George slunk around to the backyard and peeked in the window. It was open a crack, and he could hear Jonathan's auntie Mary weeping. She sat at the kitchen table with her head propped in her hands. Her shoulders rocked back and forth with her sobs.

An official-looking paper lay on the table by her hand. George recognized the Hawaiian government stamp on top, but it was too far away to read. Instinctively, he knew the document was responsible for Jonathan and Alice's arrest.

Mary sat up, wiped her tears. She snatched the paper, wadded it into a ball, and threw it against the window.

Startled, George jumped back and stumbled. He smacked a large potted plant, and it knocked against the house. His elbow smarted from where it'd struck the ground.

"Who's there?" Mary's voice wavered. "Show yourself. I'm not afraid of you. I have a baseball bat, and I'll use it."

George scrambled to his feet, holding his elbow. "Don't be afraid, Miss Mary. It's me, George."

"George?" She marched to the back door and stood on the porch with her hands on her hips. "What are you doing out there at this time of night? You should be home in bed."

"Why did the police take Jonathan and Alice away?"

Her face froze and she looked frightened. She stepped back into the kitchen and started to close the door.

George pushed against it. "What's happened?"

"You shouldn't be here," Mary said. "They might come back. You go on home now."

"Wait. You have to tell me. Jonathan's my best friend."

Mary sighed, opened the door, and motioned him in. She waited until she'd bolted the lock before she spoke again. "No one can help him or Alice. It's too late."

She hurried to the window, looked out, and drew the curtains closed.

"What do you mean?" George asked. "What's happened?"

She started to bawl. George felt really uncomfortable. He'd never seen an adult so upset before, and Mary was the last person he'd expect to break down and cry.

He helped her to a chair and got her a glass of water.

"Drink this," he said and set the glass on the table.

He pulled out a chair for himself, and that's when he saw Jonathan's lucky coin on the floor. That wasn't good. Jonathan never went anywhere without it. George picked it up and rubbed his thumb on the raised Chinese writing. Maybe the coin would work for him. He closed his eyes and wished. Let the arrest be one big mistake.

Mary stopped bawling, but her face was ghost white and her eyes like black holes. She started to rock with her hands fisted over her mouth.

George spotted the paper wad she'd thrown at the window.

Without thinking, he slipped Jonathan's lucky coin into his pocket and picked up the paper. He sat across from Mary and smoothed it flat on the table. The dread in his stomach grew as he read.

CIVIL ARREST WARRANT
Date: February 24, 1946

Subjects: Jonathan Napua, age 13
Alice Napua, age 14

Address: 745 Wainee Street
Lahaina, Maui
Hawaii

Section 302 of the civil code authorizes the Board of Health the power to arrest and detain any leprous person deemed capable of spreading the disease of leprosy. It is the duty of every police, or district Justice, to deliver all said persons to the Board of Health for isolation.

The above mentioned are to be taken into custody, transported to Kalaupapa and to be quarantined until such time as they are deemed cured.

You are ordered to provide a list of all persons who have come into regular contact with above mentioned lepers. Failure to provide this information is considered a punishable crime.

Signed and authorized by,

Harold Baldwin Masuda
Minister of the Interior
President of the Board of Health

"This is crazy," George said after he struggled through the legal language of the arrest warrant. "Jonathan isn't sick. Neither is Alice. They're not . . ."

Mary lowered her hands, her face now blotched. "You're not always sick when you first get it."

"Then why lock them up?"

"Because the *lepela* is contagious. It could infect everybody. There's no cure."

"I don't believe it," George said. "It isn't true. Jonathan's not a leper. And neither is Alice."

Mary stood. "I'm afraid it is true. I saw the signs, but I didn't want to believe it. I thought if Jonathan would just wear his shirt and keep it covered, no one would notice. Like it didn't exist."

"You mean that patch of white skin on his arm? That's leprosy? That's no big deal. Just white skin. Lots of folks on the mainland have white skin. They don't lock them up."

"The patches turn into sores," she said.

He dry swallowed. Horrible things happened to people who got the disease. A chill ran down his spine.

Leprosy.

"The sores get worse and worse and worse," Mary said, and shuddered. "They'll change Jonathan and Alice's looks until we won't even recognize them."

George didn't want to think of his best friend's fingers and toes falling off. Or Alice's perfect nose.

He scraped the tiny cut on his thumb with his fingernail. It started to bleed. He wiped the blood onto his pants, suddenly not feeling well at all. Did he have Jonathan's blood running though his veins? Would he get leprosy, too?

She started to cry again. "You go home, now. Don't tell anyone you were here. And if anyone asks, pretend you've never heard of us."

Feeling sick, George left. He raced back to the Hauala stone and stuck his hand in the water. Nothing happened. Its power didn't work this time. The cut hadn't healed.

George looked at the sky. The moon had dropped low toward the horizon. The ring around it was now huge. He had to get home before morning broke or he'd be in big trouble. Pressing his forefinger to his thumb, he raced against the fading night.

Just as he reached his house, a light came on in his grandparents' bedroom window. He had to hustle.

On the back porch he kicked off his *slippahs*, opened the door a crack, and peeked into the front room. The muffled voices of Kapuna and Tutu came from their bedroom. Luckily his bedroom was close to the back door. He tiptoed inside and scooted into his room.

He had just pulled the covers over his head when his bedroom door opened.

"He's still asleep," Tutu whispered. "Should we wake him before we leave?"

"No," Kapuna answered. "Let the sun wake him, otherwise we'll have to listen to him complain about missing out on a fishing trip."

The door closed and they left him.

In spite of all that had happened, George fell into a deep sleep. He might have slept all day if not for the loud thud that shook the house, followed by the sound of breaking glass.

George sat bolt upright in bed.

Outside, the wind howled. Through his bedroom window, palm trees whipped back and forth. Storm clouds burst and rain pounded the metal roof.

George leaped out of bed and slipped on a pair of shorts. In the front room, broken glass glittered on the floor like sharp confetti. Then he saw what had wakened him. The old palm tree from the front yard had uprooted and its top smashed through the window and crushed Kapuna's chair.

Rain splattered though the broken window.

"Kapuna! Tutu!" George shouted and checked all the rooms. They should have been home by now. Had they been caught in the storm?

George raced out the back door and ran toward the beach.

Heavy rain pelted his skin and he was soaked in seconds. As he ran, he dodged the swirling debris whipped up by the wind. Several trees had snapped and lay like dead fish stranded in the aftermath of a tsunami.

When he reached the beach, giant waves smashed the shoreline. He squinted against the rain, searching for his grandfather's canoe. It was nowhere in sight.

An angry knot formed in George's stomach. Maybe Mr. Kim was right. He always said George was a curse, not only to the ground he walked on, but to everyone he loved. First to Jonathan and now his grandparents.

No, he wouldn't think about it. Instead, he'd do something.

But what?

He frowned. Bit his lower lip. Felt a sour fist-punch to his stomach when he realized his best and only real option. There just wasn't a better choice.

4

THE STORM

George pounded on Mr. Kim's back door. When his neighbor didn't come, George pounded harder. It seemed like whenever it was convenient, the old man pretended to be deaf.

"Mr. Kim! Answer the door."

The door opened a crack. "What do you want? There's too much rain for garden work today. Besides, you too late."

"My grandparents are missing. They went out in their boat before the storm and they haven't come back."

"They probably went to shore to wait out the storm. You do the same. Go home and wait."

George breathed a little easier. For once, Mr. Kim was probably right. Kapuna wasn't foolish. He wouldn't try to ride out the fury of the storm in the little outrigger. Still, there was the problem with the broken window. Tutu would be upset when she came home and found everything in the front room wet.

"There's another problem, Mr. Kim. A tree broke the window in the living room. It's raining inside."

"You fix, while you wait for them to come home."

"How?"

"You so smart. You figure it out. Maybe for once you can fix problem instead of being problem. Your grandparents should not have brought you here. You bring bad luck to them. Go home. I don't need bad luck, too."

Mr. Kim slammed the door.

George went back to the house, grumbling that Mr. Kim was a crazy old grump.

"Who does he think he is? It's not like he knows anything. I'm not bad luck." Then George thought of all that had happened in the last twenty-four hours. "Or am I?"

He hit the wall with his fist.

His best friend was a leper. And now Kapuna and Tutu were missing. Hopefully not drowned; still he couldn't tap down the fear. No, he told himself, don't think that. Don't bring them bad luck with such thoughts. Think positive. Kapuna and Tutu would come home once the storm ended.

And Tutu would be disappointed when she saw the mess in her front room. He'd take Mr. Kim's advice. He'd fix the window and clean up the rain and broken glass.

He searched for something large enough to cover the hole and came up with nothing. Then he got an idea. It wasn't the best idea, but it should work. First he went to the shed for a hammer and nails. Next he went into the bathroom and pulled down the pink flowered shower curtain. It was big and waterproof.

Now that he had his materials, he set to work. Glass crunched under his shoes. He pushed Kapuna's chair out of the way, dragged the top of the palm tree to the front door, and tossed it into the front yard. Now for the hard part. The curtain flapped and wrapped itself around George as he tried to hold it in place. The wind tugged it one way, and then another. But once he got the top edge nailed, it was easy.

George stepped back to admire his work. Nailed in place, the pink curtain was the perfect size. It wavered and bulged like the wind was breathing life into it. He didn't know how long it would hold, but at least it kept the rain out for now. Next he swept up the broken glass and mopped the floor. By the time he finished, the storm had been carried away on the Trade Winds and the sky was a bright blue.

He went back to the beach and ran north and south, searching for a sign of his grandparents.

"Kapuna! Tutu!" he shouted until his throat felt raw.

He spotted Kapuna's canoe, or what was left of it, on the beach. The knot returned to his stomach. He ran toward to it. A huge hole gaped in the bottom, and the outrigger had snapped off. George traced his fingers over the carved sea turtle design on the hull. It was the same turtle design as his father's necklace.

Please let Mr. Kim be right for once, George thought. Kapuna and Tutu had to have gone to shore to wait out the storm. They couldn't have drowned. While they were on shore, their boat must have blown back out to sea, not them.

George raced back to Mr. Kim's.

"What you want now?" Mr. Kim asked.

"I found Kapuna's canoe. Part of it washed up on the beach. Kapuna and Tutu must be stranded, like you said. Please, can you take your truck out to look for them?"

Mr. Kim frowned.

"I'll weed your garden every week for a year."

"Okay, but I do this for your grandmother and grandfather. Not for you."

Mr. Kim went for his keys, and George went to wait at the pickup. He opened the passenger door, and before he could get in, a wet Poi Dog leaped into the seat. Great, he'd have to sit on a wet seat. George ordered the dog out, but without success. He was pulling on the dog's collar when Mr. Kim came out.

"Leave Poi Dog alone. You sit in back," Mr. Kim said. "Poi Dog rides up front with me."

Mr. Kim got in and started the engine. George climbed on the bed of the pickup truck, thinking at least he wouldn't have to listen to Mr. Kim's complaints.

Mr. Kim shouted out his window. "We go north to look. If they are south, someone from town will find them."

George stood leaning against the cab and held on to keep his balance. He grinned, not a happy grin, but a tight one. Poi Dog had done him a favor. Standing gave him a better view of the shoreline than if he'd ridden up front.

A lot of junk littered the road, blown down by the storm. Mr. Kim had to steer around trees, branches, and sections of tin roofs. They stopped every half mile or so. Mr. Kim waited behind the wheel while a hopeful George and the dog ran up and down each new section of beach.

Each time, George returned to the truck disappointed.

After two hours, Mr. Kim said, "It's getting dark. Their boat not come this far north. We go back."

"We can't stop looking now." What was wrong with Mr. Kim? Didn't he realize it was too soon to give up the search? "Kapuna or Tutu could be hurt."

It was useless to argue with the old man.

Mr. Kim started the truck and made a U-turn. George couldn't believe it. Mr. Kim was driving off. Quitting the search. If George didn't hustle, he'd be stranded ten miles from home. He raced after the pickup and hopped on the tailgate just before Mr. Kim shifted into second gear.

When they reached the turnoff for their street, Mr. Kim kept driving toward town.

George leaned forward and shouted in the window. "Where are we going?"

Mr. Kim ignored the question. He drove down Front Street, turned down a side street and parked in front of the police station. He got out and motioned for George to join him on the sidewalk.

"We make report. Police can look for grandparents. Okay?"

"Okay." What else could George say? Besides, it did make sense. At the same time, he felt uneasy. Kapuna always said it was better to avoid the police than to invite their attention.

George reluctantly followed Mr. Kim into the station. The desk sergeant asked them to wait. Twenty minutes later, a policeman called Mr. Kim's name and led them back to his desk. He held out his hand to Mr. Kim. "Hello. I'm Sergeant Cole. I understand you have a missing person report to file."

Mr. Kim, for once in his life, didn't say anything. He let George tell the officer about the ill-fated fishing trip, the wrecked boat. George ended with, "My grandparents could be hurt. You have to find them."

"The storm has done a lot of damage around town," the sergeant said and sighed. "Your grandparents are the fourth missing persons reported in the last hour. We'll do our best."

"Good," Mr. Kim said and stood up. "I can go home now."

The policeman wrote a few final notes on a form and then asked, "So the boy will be with you until we find his grandparents?"

"With me?" Mr. Kim said. "No. No. The boy bring bad luck. Take him to someone else. His friend's house. They live in town."

"That okay with you?" the policeman asked George.

"Uh . . ." George hesitated. Miss Mary had said to forget he knew them. "No. They aren't home. They moved."

The sergeant turned to Mr. Kim. "Are you sure you can't take him to your house?"

"No. I see his friend yesterday. He live here in town."

"Not any more," George said. "That was his last day in Lahaina. They moved up-country. To Kula."

"Then, young man, I guess you'll have to stay here with us," the sergeant said. "I'll contact child welfare."

"Can't I just go home? My grandparents will be worried if they come home and I'm missing."

"How are old are you?"

"Fifteen-and-a-half," George lied, hoping Mr. Kim wouldn't contradict him. He was tall and could easily pass for fifteen, maybe sixteen.

"Let me check with the captain."

The sergeant returned five minutes later with a man George recognized. His mouth went dry. It was one of the policemen who had arrested Jonathan and Alice.

"This is Captain Yamaguchi. He has a few questions for you, George."

"Hello, George. Your last name is Kahula? A friend of Jonathan Napua?"

George swallowed and shook his head.

"Mrs. Osaka, Jonathan Napua's seventh grade teacher, tells me that his best friend's name is George Kahula."

"It must be a different George Kahula. I'm in high school."

"Don't believe this boy," Mr. Kim said. "He lies. He go to elementary school and he has friend named Jonathan. They trampled my garden yesterday. You keep him here. He's bad news."

George looked at his feet. He swallowed hard and wondered why Mr. Kim hated him so much.

"Until we get this sorted out," Captain Yamaguchi said, "put this boy in room one. He's on the Department of Health's detainment list."

What? George dry swallowed again. Did they think he was a leper? That was impossible. Or was it? He rubbed his thumb.

"Follow me," Sergeant Cole said. He led George to a small windowless room with just one chair sitting in a corner.

"Sir?"

"You just sit there and wait."

"I have to go to the bathroom."

The sergeant closed the door like he hadn't heard George.

George slumped in the chair. In less than a day, his whole life was ruined. Maybe Mr. Kim was right. Maybe he was bad luck. Maybe that was the real reason his grandparents' boat had been wrecked in the storm.

George felt like crying, but he was too old for that. Only babies cried. He blinked hard and pinched his leg. He had to get out of there. He couldn't let them turn him over to the Health Department.

The door opened. The sergeant handed George a red coffee can.

"What's this?" George asked, feeling a faint flicker of hope. Maybe he could escape and continue the search for is grandparents.

"You said you had to go to the bathroom."

"I can't do what I need to do in that," George said. "I need a toilet."

The sergeant groaned. "Then come with me and be quick about it. I have work to do. Don't have time to baby-sit."

The bathroom was a one-seater at the rear of the building. George went in and closed the door, wishing it had a lock.

At least the sergeant hadn't come in with him.

Moonlight partially lit the room through a high, narrow window over the sink. It was small, but not so small that George couldn't wriggle through it if he tried.

He hoped it wasn't nailed shut.

He stood on the sink, lifted the latch and pushed up. The window was stuck. He pushed harder. It squeaked as it inched open. George froze. Had the sergeant heard?

"What's taking so long in there?"

"I'm almost done."

George flushed the toilet with his foot and used all his strength to push open the window. Without thinking, he dove through the opening head-first and got stuck. He dangled half in and half out of the room.

The bathroom door opened.

George frantically wriggled forward a few inches. The windowsill dug into his ribs, scraping his stomach. Using his hands, he pushed against the outside wall, trying to propel himself through the narrow opening. He'd almost made it when two large hands clamped on his ankles. His *slippahs* fell off, and he felt himself being roughly dragged back into the building.

5

THE ESCAPE

George struggled to free his feet from the policeman's iron grip. He was still half in and half out of the little window over the sink.

"Stop kicking," the officer yelled.

George's foot slammed into what he thought was the man's nose. The impact made a sickening crunch. George didn't have time to feel squeamish. He had to get out of there.

The man swore.

George power-kicked again.

The man let go, and George popped through the window, diving face-first into the street.

"Stop that boy," the policeman howled in a muffled voice.

George jumped up and raced down the deserted alley, ignoring the sharp pain in his right knee. When he reached Front Street, he ran north. Up ahead, a large crowd of men had gathered under the fifty-foot banyan tree in front of the old courthouse. The huge old tree covered the whole city block.

He ran for the crowd, hoping it would be impossible for the police to spot him. More than two hundred men dressed in the rough clothes of cane workers listened to a man perched on a wooden box near the main trunk of the tree.

No one noticed George as he wormed his way into the middle of the mob. Sweat trickled down his neck as he brushed past a man reeking of tobacco smoke.

"They said when the war was over our wages would be raised and our work hours shortened. They lied!" the speaker shouted.

Men cheered.

"We're not slaves. We are honest men. If we stick together, they will be forced to meet our demands."

More cheers.

"The time has come for personal sacrifice. We must strike until Baldwin offers every man $1.50 for a ten-hour work day!"

One man shouted from the crowd, "The police are coming!"

George's heartbeat raced. He dry swallowed. He couldn't let them catch him now. Not when he was almost free.

The speaker shook his fist in the air. "Hold your ground. Conditions won't change if we don't fight."

The crowd began to panic and break apart, fractured into clumps of men hurrying away from the demonstration. George pushed into a small group of leather-skinned men rapidly exiting the square. They cast worried looks at the police officers entering the crowd.

"We can't afford to strike," muttered one red-faced man. He was large, and George stuck close like he was the man's shadow.

"You got that right," said another. "They'll just bring in replacement workers and we'll lose our jobs."

The men rounded the remains of a coral wall and headed to a battered pickup truck. Three men squeezed into the cab and six more piled into the back, leaving George on the sidewalk alone. Panicked, he shot a glance over his shoulder. Sergeant Cole was headed his way.

"You need a ride?" one man asked.

"Yeah," George said and leaped in.

The truck started with a bang.

Sergeant Cole started to run toward them.

"Step on it!" the red-faced worker hollered to the driver. "The police are after us."

The truck lurched forward.

"Faster," the man yelled.

The truck squealed over cobbles and raced out of town.

"We've lost him!"

The men in back cheered. George breathed a sigh of relief. He'd made it. He was safe.

"Where are you from, boy?" the red-faced man asked.

Revved up that that he'd just avoided arrest, George forgot and told the truth. "Just north of town."

"Let me know when we're close. I'll tell my friend to stop."

They were almost to George's house and he was about to ask the man to stop when he saw the dark silhouette of an unfamiliar car parked out front. The red glow of a cigarette flipped from the car. Not fair, thought George. It looked like the police were watching his house.

He waited another quarter of a mile before he said, "We're almost there."

The red-faced man pounded on the truck cab and the driver pulled to a stop.

"Thanks for the ride."

George waited until the truck was out of sight before he back-tracked toward his house. Was it safe to return, or was he being stupid?

If only Kapuna and Tutu were home. They wouldn't let the police take him. But he knew they weren't there. Fear laced with sorrow wormed its way into his heart. The sea had claimed them, and he was on his own. A tear trickled down his cheek and he swiped it with the back of his hand. He didn't have time to grieve. Or feel sorry for himself. He was on his own.

Okay. He'd go underground and make his way to Molokai, find his parents and hope they would be glad to see him.

For a trip like that, he'd need supplies. Going back to the house was a risk he'd have to take.

Cutting between two houses, he ran to the beach. Crouched low like a soldier on reconnaissance, he approached his home from the rear. The grass felt wet on his feet as he crept into the backyard. He eased closer and used the shed as cover.

No telltale lights inside. No movements or sound. His fingers felt in his pocket for Jonathan's coin and he rubbed it for luck. He'd need luck if he was get in and out of the house without being caught.

Out front, the squawk of a police radio broke the silence, followed by low urgent words murmured into a microphone. A car engine started. George scooted to the side of the house in time to see the car's headlights sweep the front lawn as the car backed into the street. It took off.

Tension drained from his tight muscles. Taking a deep breath, he half-smiled. He was safe. At least for the moment.

Poi Dog barked once and ran toward him.

"Shhhh," George hissed. The police were gone, but that didn't mean Mr. Kim wouldn't call them back if he thought George was in the house. The dog trotted over. George patted its head.

When Mr. Kim didn't appear, George inched his way to the back door and went inside. Poi Dog whined on the porch. George let the dog in and whispered, "Be a good boy. No barks."

Inside, it was too quiet. No one was home, and, like the house, George felt empty and alone. The shower curtain over the front window breathed in and out with the night breeze. George's own breath came out in short and low pants accompanied by the clicking of Poi Dog's toenails on the floor.

He grimaced. It wasn't fair. Not right that Kapuna and Tutu were gone, drowned at sea. He fought back tears.

He grabbed a duffle bag from the closet and went into the kitchen. Poi Dog sniffed the garbage while George raided the pantry. Six cans of Spam, half a loaf of bread, and some cheese went into the bag. At least he wouldn't starve. The grocery money Tutu kept in the sugar bowl went into his back pocket. It felt like stealing, but it wasn't. It belonged to him now. His grandparents were dead.

And he was an orphan.

No. That wasn't true. Suddenly he felt the first bit of hope. He wasn't an orphan. He had parents. He just had to find them. To do that he needed the letter from his parents he'd read the night before. Was it only last night? It seemed like it was months ago.

Where had Tutu put it?

He found the envelope on the dresser in his grandparents' room next to their wedding picture. Poi Dog jumped up and knocked over a small bottle of perfume. Tutu's scent flooded the room. He grabbed the letter and shoved it in his pocket. Lights from a passing car flashed in the room. He ducked and cautiously peeked out the window. The street was empty, but an uneasy feeling came over him. He had to leave. To get out of the house, right now.

He raced to his bedroom, Poi Dog at his heels. He slipped his father's turtle necklace over his neck and wrapped his parents' picture in some clothes before stowing it in the duffle with the food. Before closing the back door, he slid on Kapuna's extra pair of *slippahs.* They felt big and comfortable, like Kapuna.

George knew he shouldn't take them. That if he kept them, it would delay his grandfather's spirit journey to the afterlife of Po.

"Kapuna, Tutu, I know your spirits must still be here. Kapuna, please forgive me for taking the *slippahs,* but I'm just borrowing them. Please wait for me at Puukekaa before you leave this world. I'm coming. I need your help."

Shouldering the duffel, he slunk out the back door and headed for the beach. Poi Dog ran after him.

"Go home," George told the dog. The mutt was the last thing he needed if he wanted to be invisible.

Poi Dog whined and jumped on George.

George squatted and rubbed the dog's ears. "Listen, you can't come with me. What would Mr. Kim do without you? No one else likes him. You have to stay, and I have to leave. I'm not coming back."

It was as if the words had sealed his fate. Whatever happened next, his life would never be the same. There was no time to waste. He had to get to Puukekaa before Kapuna and Tutu left for Po.

He stood and using a stern voice said, "Stay."

He'd walk the four miles north and hope the police didn't find him. If he had a canoe, he could paddle the distance in about the same time it'd take to walk.

Poi Dog seemed to read George's mind. He yipped and ran toward Mr. Kim's garage and the silhouette of his master's canoe. Mr. Kim hardly ever used it. Not once in the last year, and he'd never miss it. Besides, Mr. Kim owed it to him. If it weren't for the cranky old man, George wouldn't be on the run.

Poi Dog barked.

"Shhhhhhh."

And it wouldn't be stealing, rationalized George. Poi Dog had all but given him permission to liberate the canoe.

George tossed the duffel into the boat. Grabbing the front, he dragged the canoe toward the beach. Poi Dog ran back and forth between the ocean and George. The canoe was small, but it was slow going over the sand. George had to stop twice to catch his breath before he reached the water.

Poi Dog jumped into the canoe and sat up front.

"No!" George whisper-shouted, "I told you, you can't come. Out!"

George grabbed a can of Spam and opened it. It smelled like ham. Wonderful, salty ham, and he was starving. It had been a long day, and he hadn't eaten in hours. He broke off a piece and shoved it in his mouth.

Poi Dog began to slobber.

George ate another chunk. "It's good stuff, Poi Dog. You'd really like it."

He held out a piece to tease the dog and then dropped it in the sand. Poi Dog jumped out, and George shoved the boat into the water. It floated. He hopped in and paddled hard. As soon as he was beyond the breaking waves, he headed north.

The night air was warm. Sweat glistened on his arms.

It was easy to follow the dark shoreline in the moonlight. The water was a dark inky blue. Fluorescent white waves marked the submerged rocks dangerously close to the surface.

At first his arms ached, but then he hit his stride and his energy surged. He felt like he could paddle all night. It wasn't long before he spotted Puukekaa. The rock jutted into the sky, eighty-five feet high. It was the most eastern point on Maui—the leaping-off place of the soul. The place where his grandparents' spirits would leave this world for the afterlife.

He hoped he wasn't too late. That taking the *slippahs* had delayed their departure. That he was in time to reach Kapuna and Tutu's spirits before they left this world.

The rock loomed closer and closer until its shadow blotted out the reflected moonlight on the water. He was almost there. Forty feet from shore, the boat scraped the reef and stopped.

Any other time he would have jumped in the water and lifted the boat off the reef, but the waves were rough, and he couldn't risk losing his precious cargo. Without money and food, he'd never make it to Molokai.

George stood and tried to rock the canoe free. Using his paddle, he pried at the lava. It didn't work. A huge wave hit the canoe. He staggered, and his legs flew from under him. He landed hard on his back.

Another wave hit and he heard the outrigger snap. He felt the boat shudder as it scraped on the submerged rock. He sat up and fought to control the boat as it shot forward. Water swirled through the floorboards. In seconds, the seawater rose from his ankles to his knees.

George grabbed for the duffel, but a wave sucked it out of reach. In shock, he watched the sea devour the Spam, clothes, and the photograph. Too late. He plunged in for the bag, but it was gone. He dove again and again, but it was hopeless in the dark. Kapuna's *slippahs* floated on the surface. He grabbed them, shoved them into the waistband of his shorts and swam for shore.

Maybe Mr. Kim had been right. George was cursed. Everything he cared about was lost. Everyone he loved was gone, and everything he needed to get him to Molokai was at the bottom of the sea.

He staggered out of the water.

The shadow of Puukekaa loomed over him. Maybe everything wasn't lost. Maybe the stories of Po were true and he was in time to catch Kapuna and Tutu's spirits before they left this world. He still had Kapuna's *slippahs*, and his grandfather couldn't leave without them.

Barefoot, he climbed the rock, ignoring the sharp stabs of the lava.

"Kapuna? Tutu? I've come to see you off and to ask for guidance."

He reached the top and waited, hoping to feel their presence. The night breeze whispered over his skin. The stars glinted in the dark sky, seeming to mock him and knowing that he'd never really believed the legends of his ancestors, like Jonathan had. But the healing powers of the Hauola stone had worked. Maybe Puukekaa really was the leaping place of souls. And if it was true, he could see his grandparents one last time.

He waited, praying that something would happen. Desperate for the spirits of Kapuna and Tutu to appear.

"Kapuna, I know you haven't left yet. I still have your *slippahs* and I know you can't leave if I keep them." George held up the sandals. "Maybe you need them to walk in where you're going. I'm giving them back."

George flung the *slippahs* with a hard underhanded pitch and lost his balance. He fell feet first toward the pounding waves. It felt like he dropped in slow motion; almost as if invisible arms cuddled him. The air caressed his ears. He tasted the spray of sea salt. A wave broke directly beneath him, and then he plunged into a cushion of white froth.

The sea sucked him deep into its belly. George didn't fight, but let himself be consumed. What did it matter? He was cursed. And he probably had leprosy, too. It was just a matter of time before his fingers and toes fell off. Like Jonathan's. But If Jonathan was there, he'd yell at George for being a total idiot.

Survival instincts kicked in, and he fought his way to the surface. He swam against the current and away from the dangerous rocks that would shred his skin and bring sharks. Safe for the moment, he bobbed on the surface and coughed up sea water. Then he realized he was being dragged out to sea. Caught in a riptide.

Don't panic, he told himself. Swim across the current. He did. When he felt free, he treaded water to catch his breath before heading for shore. Exhausted, he swam and then let the waves help him onto the sandy beach. He crawled out of the water on his hands and knees and collapsed. Water lapped at his feet. His last thought before he lost consciousness was that he was alone.

Sometime later, he felt something poke his ribs.

"Go away," he said. "Leave me alone."

6

NEW PLAN

George felt another jab in his ribs and winced. He turned onto his back and blinked hard.

An old woman leaned on a carved walking stick, her long gray hair fluttering in wisps about her shoulders. She faced the sea as if she hadn't noticed him lying at her feet. He stared up at her profile and saw that her left eye was a milky white. She must be blind, he thought, and at the same moment saw the muscles on her arm bunch. She raised the stick and jabbed down again with a vicious force. He rolled away and jumped up.

"It's time you moved," she said, her voice low and raspy like it had worn out years earlier. She turned to face George, her right eye dark and glittering.

He gaped. Large black tattoos covered the left side of her face, continued down her neck and emerged from the hem of her faded muumuu.

Had he drowned and gone to Po? That thought disappeared when she poked his foot with her stick.

"Ouch!" he yelped and hopped on one foot.

"You are too young to jump off Puukekaa," she said.

"I didn't jump. I fell." He swiped damp sand from his face. "Who are you?"

"You need something to eat, something to make you feel alive. Your ancestors are not ready to receive you." She turned and trudged up the beach, leaning heavily on her walking stick.

Who was this strange woman? And how had she known he'd fallen off Puukekaa? It had to have been hours ago. Her talk of food made him realize he was starved and he wondered, had it been an invitation or friendly advice? He was trying to decide which when she paused and looked back.

"You coming?" she called.

He hesitated. She seemed strange, but his stomach rumbled, urging him to trust her. After all, she was just an old woman and didn't look anything close to a police officer. He hurried after her. Every muscle felt stiff, and the dried salt water pulled at his skin, tightening it like a pair of too-small jeans.

They walked in silence until they arrived at a small one-room shed. It overlooked the sea at the edge of a sugar cane field recently cut bare and burned. The smell of damp ashes still singed the air.

Eight outrigger canoes in various conditions were scattered about the yard. The small shed faced the ocean. Near the door a wicker chair, two wooden boxes and a small table had been placed around an outdoor fire pit. Cool, thought George, an outside living room. It wouldn't matter if you spilled Coke on the floor, and you'd never have to sweep or mop it up.

The woman motioned George to sit on one of the wooden boxes.

He sat and found himself staring at her tattoos even though he knew it was rude. They seemed to come alive when she spoke or moved. The intricate patterns reminded him of pictures he'd seen in a *National Geographic* at school.

He wanted to ask her about the tattoos, but instead he asked, "Who are you?"

The woman didn't answer. Seeming to ignore him, she stirred the coals of the fire pit, added some wood, and went into the shed. By the time she returned with two frying pans, the fire had kindled. She set the pans on a blackened grate over the flames; gravy in one, a thick hamburger patty in the other. In no time at all, the meat spurted and the gravy bubbled.

George could already taste it. It smelled so good. His stomach rumbled, and to his embarrassment, his mouth watered like Poi Dog's.

She flipped the meat with a fork, pushed it to the side of the pan, and added a generous spoonful of cooked rice. The savory smells mingled and tortured George. He felt so hungry his stomach ached.

The woman didn't speak. She poked the meat, stirred the gravy, and turned the rice until she was satisfied it was ready. First she scooped the rice onto a metal plate, then plopped the meat on top and covered it with the gravy. She handed the plate to George.

The plate was hot and almost burned his fingers, but he didn't care.

"You're not eating?" George said, trying to sound polite, but hoping he wouldn't have to share.

"Ate my breakfast hours ago," she said and sat in the high-back wicker chair across the fire. She looked almost regal.

George ate fast like a mangy mongrel. When he realized his plate was almost empty, he forced himself to slow and to chew each bite. When he was finished, he looked up. The woman leaned on her stick and studied George with her good eye.

"Thanks," he said. "That was the best *Loco Moco* I've ever had."

"Tell me, boy. What business brought you to Puukekaa Rock?"

"I . . ." George started to spin a lie about how he wanted to become an Olympic high diver one day, but caught himself. Something about the woman's penetrating stare stopped him, and the story of the storm and his grandparents spilled out. In the end, he told her more than he'd meant to, but not about the police or his own fear of leprosy.

"So what is your plan?" she asked. "What will you do now?"

"I'm going to Molokai to find my parents."

She nodded her approval.

"How much would you want for that canoe?" George asked, pointing to the smallest outrigger.

"How much do you have?"

"Fifteen dollars," George said.

"You may have the boat for ten dollars."

Overjoyed, George reached into his back pocket. The money was gone. His heart sank as he frantically checked his other pockets. His father's letter was still in his right front pocket. In the left pocket his fingers closed on Jonathan's lucky coin.

"It's gone," he said. "All I have is this, but . . ." He held up the lucky coin.

"It's not yours to give," she finished for him. "You will have to earn the money."

"Do you have a job for me?"

"No, I have no money to pay you for work."

"You can pay me with the canoe."

The woman shook her head. "That was not our deal. The deal is that I will give you the canoe when you give me ten dollars."

George put his face in his hands and shook his head. The curse had followed him from the rock. It just wasn't fair. What would he do now?

"You must find work," she said. "Work that will make you strong enough to paddle the Pailolo Straits."

George dropped his hands and slumped. "Where would I find a job? No one would hire me."

"Replacement workers are needed in the cane. The workers are striking. Even though the Big Five has brought in Filipino Sadakas, more workers are still needed. A resourceful boy won't have a problem talking himself into a job."

George tried to think of a better option, but couldn't.

She seemed to sense George's conclusion and stood as if to dismiss him. "When you have the money, come back for the canoe."

"It's a deal," he said.

"The sooner you go, the sooner you'll earn the money."

George started across the field, both disappointed and hopeful. When he reached the main road, he reluctantly turned south in the direction of Lahaina. The strong unpleasant odor of sugar processing greeted him long before he saw the mill. Its unsettling sweet stench grew stronger with every step, and by the time he reached the mill, he was breathing through his mouth. He remembered Kapuna once say, the smell of cooking cane was the smell of money.

A long line of men wound its way into a long squat building next to the mill.

"That the job line?" George asked a man who sat behind the wheel of a truck loaded down with cut sugar cane.

The man nodded.

George hurried to the end of the line. He was nervous, afraid they wouldn't hire him because he was only thirteen. He'd pretend to be older. Tell them that he was short for his age. The men in front of him were not much taller than him. They jabbered in a language George couldn't understand. Were they the Filipino Sadakas the old woman had mentioned?

He fingered his father's necklace and stood straighter, tried to look taller and older. With so many men in front of him, he just knew he wouldn't be hired. More men queued behind him.

The line moved forward at a quick pace. Near the door he realized that men came out almost as fast as they went in. The exiting men all wore broad smiles and had metal tags, kind of like army dogtags, but bigger.

Finally it was George's turn. Inside it was hot and stuffy. Men's sweat blended with the sugar-processing odor.

"Next!"

George stepped up to the counter. A stern-looking woman in black glasses stared at his disheveled appearance. She reminded him of his teacher, and he found himself smoothing his hair with his hand.

"Name?" Her voice sounded bored.

George hesitated. Should he give her his real name?

She looked up from her paperwork. "You old enough to work?"

George smiled, in spite of his queasy stomach. "I'm short for my age. I'm sixteen."

"Okay then, name?"

He said the first name that popped into his mind. "George James."

"You read and write?"

George nodded.

She pushed a paper at him. "Fill out this form and take it to the man at the desk."

George carefully printed his assumed name and age. He tried to write smaller, less neat so it wouldn't look like a school boy's handwriting.

He left the address space blank.

When it was his turn, he handed the form to the round-faced man. The man wore a dark suit and was all smiles.

"Thank you." The man scanned the form. "Where do you live?"

"I've just come from Hana. I need a job before I can pay rent."

"Do you have any experience?"

"My family had a farm," George said, which was not exactly a lie. The man didn't need to know it was before George was born.

The man made a few notations.

"I'm a fast learner," George said. "I'm strong and can work hard."

"Well, if it's hard work you want, I can offer you a position in the cane fields. That suit you?"

"Yes, sir," George said, afraid the man might change his mind.

The man stamped the form and handed George a slip of paper.

"Give this to the clerk by the door. He'll give you a *Bango Tag* with your worker number on it. Don't lose it."

"Thank you, sir. Where do I report to work? And when do I start?"

"The clerk will assign you a field foreman. Any more questions?"

"How much will I get paid?"

"You'll start at fifty cents a day. If you can put out a man's worth of labor, we'll double it."

George did the math. At fifty cents a day, that would be three dollars a week. He smiled. This would be easy. In three and a half weeks, he'd have the money for the canoe; maybe less time if he could prove he was worth a man's wage.

7

SUGAR CANE

A white man in a Panama hat and a red shirt looked over the group of new hires. Except for George, they were all Filipinos, fresh off the boat. The man wiped his face with a red handkerchief and then blew the whistle that hung from his neck.

"Gather up over here," he shouted, waving his hands.

The men jostled to get closer, pushing George to the back of the crowd.

"My name is Mr. Davies." The man spoke slow and loud like he was talking to brain-impaired inferiors. "I am the field foreman." He waved to another worker. The man joined him. He looked like a Filipino, hunchbacked and dressed in rough work clothes. "This is Quidilla. He is my voice to you."

Quidilla nodded. In rapid fire, he translated for the men who didn't speak English. In spite of his small stature, his voice was deep and rich.

"In the field, I'm king," Mr. Davies went on. "You work hard and we'll get along just fine. Make sure you carry your *Bango Tag* at all times. It is your train ticket. Your settlement-camp pass. Your work pass. And store pass. But most important come pay day—no tag, no pay."

Did Mr. Davies say train ticket? This was great. George had never been on a train before, and now he was getting paid to ride one. Having a job wasn't so bad. He wore the new work shoes they'd given him and had new thick gloves shoved in his back pocket. The clerk had insisted George needed both because the sharp cane barbs could cut skin like butter.

He wished Jonathan was there and frowned. In his excitement over the train ride, he'd forgotten why he was there. Suddenly he felt alone in a sea of men jabbering words he couldn't understand. Stay focused, he chided himself. Earn the money for the canoe. Sail to Molokai. Find his parents, and everything would be fine.

The train engine whistled. Down the track a cloud of steam rushed toward the factory. It was exciting. It would be his first train ride. He clutched the *Bango Tag* in his pocket next to Jonathan's lucky coin.

The train's wheels screeched as it slowed.

Mr. Davies yelled, "Climb aboard."

Men surged onto the car like sharks in a feeding frenzy. George climbed the hot metal ladder and moved to the front of the car. The engine chuffed, and the car jerked forward. George almost lost his balance and instinctively grabbed a man's arm. It was Quidilla, the translator.

"Sorry," George said.

"It's okay. One day I may need to lean on you." Quidilla's eyes sparkled, and his broad smile revealed two missing teeth.

Up close, George couldn't help but notice the man's funny-shaped ears. They looked like miniature cauliflowers under his straw hat.

The man held out his hand to George. "I'm Quidilla."

George shook the man's hand, but when he tried to pull his hand back, the man held it like a fortune teller.

"This is your first day. Be glad that it is a half day, for the work is hard for one so young."

George stood straighter, towering over the hunchbacked man. "I'm sixteen. I can work hard."

"Don't be insulted. To be young and healthy is a good thing. Look at me, I'm thirty-nine and I look like an old man. My back is bent. My hands scarred."

"Quidilla! Get over here," shouted Mr. Davies. "Organize these men. I need to record their worker numbers."

George was last in line to hand over his tag. He dropped it at Mr. Davies' feet. The man swore. George scrambled to pick it up.

"Sorry."

The man stared at George and shook his head.

He turned to Quidilla and muttered, just loud enough for George to hear. "Now they're sending me kids? How do they expect me to meet the quotas if I don't have decent workers?"

George bristled at the foreman's harsh words. Well, he'd show Mr. Davies. He'd do twice the work of any man.

Quidilla caught George's eye and winked. A few minutes later, he appeared at George's side and handed him a short length of twine.

"What's this for?" George asked.

"Your *Bango Tag*. They'll charge you for another one if you lose it."

"Thanks," George said. He threaded the twine through a hole in the tag and tied it to his belt loop with a double knot.

The train tracks ran down a corridor between the fields of cane. This was going to be easy, George thought, watching the fields go by, some cut to bare earth, others tall and waiting for harvest. Working six days a week, the time should fly by. In no time, he'd have the ten dollars for the canoe.

The train slowed to a stop.

Mr. Davies blew his whistle, like a playground attendant at school. "Everybody off, time's a-wasting," he shouted. "This field needs cutting!"

The workers lined up for job assignments. As usual, George was last. Several men in front of him were handed machetes. They immediately began chopping. A wide swath of tall cane stalks toppled to the ground. That's what I want to do, thought George. Hack cane.

George slipped on his gloves. They felt clumsy and hot. It would be a little awkward holding a machete, but he'd get used to it.

When George's turn came, Mr. Davies pointed to the erratic line of carriers already lugging bundles of cut cane to the railroad track. The men looked like ants carrying impossibly large foliage on their backs.

"You start as a carrier."

"But, sir, I'm real good with a machete. I want to be a cutter."

"And I want to be a millionaire." The man spit tobacco juice on George's new shoe. "If you want to work here, you're a carrier!"

George hustled into the field.

He waited while a cane cutter threw long poles of cut cane onto a rope. When the heap reached George's waist, the cutter moved on to start another pile. George twisted the rope around the cane like he'd watched other carriers do. Something went wrong as he slung the bundle onto his back. The cane cascaded into a heap.

Mr. Davies swore loud enough for everyone to hear. "Retie that load and get it moved pronto or you'll be looking for a new job, boy!"

"Let me show you," Quidilla said as he helped George reassemble the bundle. "Put a knot on each end of the rope, it'll make it easier to handle. Now, grab both ends and wrap them around your wrists. Make sure it's tight before you hoist it onto your back."

Quidilla helped the boy flip the bundle onto his back.

George winced as the full weight of the bundle dropped on him and the cane dug into his back. The rope cut into his hand, but this time he didn't let go. Cane barbs poked his ears. He staggered to a rail car, dropped his load and rubbed his right ear. His hand came away streaked with blood.

"Keep moving," Mr. Davies shouted. "This isn't the Boy Scouts."

Quidilla was a cutter when he wasn't translating. He motioned for George to work with him, and as the day wore on, he made the bundles smaller. Still, George didn't know what hurt worse— his back, hands or ears. He trudged between the cutters and the rail line all afternoon, until he wasn't sure if he was dead or alive.

When the foreman's whistle finally sounded, George could hardly move. Quidilla boosted the boy onto the railcar.

"You did pretty well for your first day."

"I feel like I'm going to die," George said.

Quidilla helped George down when they reached the plantation camp. "You can stay with me."

———

"Why don't you go home? I'm sure that whatever you did, your parents will forgive you."

"I have no home," George said. "I have to work."

"I see." Quidilla handed a plate of rice and vegetables to George. "I would want my son to come home. What's that turtle necklace you wear?"

George's hand went to the smooth carved turtle hanging at his neck. "This was my father's," he said. "Now it's mine."

"It is good for a son to have a piece of his father."

"Do you have a son?" George asked.

"In Manila. I have a wife and two sons. When I have earned enough to buy a house and my sons an education, I will return to my family."

"I never liked school that much," George said. "But it's easier than hauling cane."

"Can you read and write?" Quidilla asked, looking hopeful.

George nodded.

"Will you write to my family for me?"

"Yes, but I don't know your language. I can only read and write in English."

"That's okay. There is a man in my village who can read English."

George tried to listen but he was exhausted and fell asleep where he sat, his plate slipping from his lap. That night he dreamed of Kapuna and Tutu. They urged him to stay strong. Not to give up.

The next morning, he awoke to Quidilla shaking his shoulder.

"Wake up, boy. The train will be here soon."

George groaned. Every inch of his body screamed in protest.

Quidilla shoved a cup of hot tea in his hand. "Drink this. You'll feel better."

George sipped the tea.

"Hurry. Drink it down. We can't be late."

George groaned. He just wanted to lie back down and sleep.

"Today will be a full day," Quidilla said and handed George a tin can. "Take this. It's your lunch."

George collapsed before lunch. He'd only lasted three hours.

At noon, a whistle blasted in his ear and he was jerked awake. Mr. Davies stood before him with a wicked grin. "No pay for you today. Get out of my sight. You're bad for morale."

"But I carried forty loads of cane."

"And these other men carried four hundred."

"I need this job. Please don't fire me."

"Okay, I'm in a good mood today. You have three days to prove you can work like a man. If not, you're gone for good."

Quidilla came over, sat down, and ate his lunch.

"What did Mr. Davies say?" he asked.

George told him.

"You go rest, tomorrow you'll feel better."

George wished he could quit. Give up. But he couldn't. He had to earn the money for the canoe. It was his only hope of ever finding his parents on Molokai.

8

HARD WORK

George didn't collapse until three on Thursday.

Friday, he managed to work the whole day because Quidilla and the other cutters prepared smaller bundles. By Saturday, he grew less sore and felt himself becoming stronger. The words of the tattooed woman came back to him, *find work that will make you strong enough to paddle the Pailolo Straits.* Well, he'd found such work and now knew he could survive, both the work and Mr. Davies.

The days slipped into the familiar pattern of work. Evenings Quidilla and George swapped stories. Quidilla talked about his family in the Philippines. George made up stories about life on a cattle ranch in Hana, imagined memories straight from a western movie he and Jonathan had watched a lifetime ago.

It was his second Saturday working, and George looked forward to having his first real day off. The previous Sunday he'd slept all day. Tomorrow, Quidilla was going to show him how to make fishing lures from plant parts.

He hardly noticed the sugar cane digging into his back anymore. His muscles had hardened, leaving his mind free to daydream. His escape to Molokai. The reunion with his parents. Would his father love him as much as Quidilla loved his sons?

George would miss Quidilla. He'd have to tell Quidilla he was leaving, but not yet. There were still two weeks until payday.

An agonized cry of pain pulled George back to the present. He turned. A man writhed on the ground, blood spurting from a gash on his leg. Quidilla was there first, pressing his hands to the wound to stop the bleeding. The other workers crowded around, helpless.

"Move out of the way!" Mr. Davies shouted, striding through the crowd of men. "Give me your shirt," he ordered George.

George slipped it off. Mr. Davies grabbed the blood-stained machete from the ground, slit the shirt and tossed both pieces to Quidilla. The Filipino used one half for a tourniquet. He bound the gash with the other.

"You, you, and you," Mr. Davies said. "Carry him to the truck. Boy, I want to talk to you."

George frowned.

"The rest of you get back to work!"

What did the foreman want? It wasn't good to be singled out.

Mr. Davies turned to George and smiled. "You still want to be a cutter? As you can see, we've just had an opening. It pays a man's wage."

George gulped. A man's wage! Come payday, he'd have even more money than he needed for the canoe. He could pay Quidilla back for all the food.

"Ride the next load to the mill and pick up a machete from the company store. Get yourself a new shirt while you're at it. Just show them your *Bango Tag* and they'll fix you up."

Before George had a chance to share his good news with Quidilla, the train whistle blew. George sprinted past the overloaded cars and jumped onto the train engine. The conductor waved him inside and let George pull the whistle. It was great. He was getting paid to play hooky from work.

The ride seemed like it was over before it started. He hopped off and ran to the company store.

"Mr. Davies sent me," he told the clerk, a smiling older man. "I need a machete and a new shirt."

"Machetes are on the back wall. Shirts are on the first aisle."

It took George longer to pick out the machete than the shirt.

"Is there anything else you'd like?"

"What? You mean I can use my *Bango Tag* for other stuff?"

"Sure thing, young man. What's your pleasure?"

George left the store wearing his new shirt and with an armload of stuff: candy bars, paper, a notebook, six pencils, candles and a couple of cans of Spam.

"I thought you'd be excited," George said. "Not that the man was hurt, but that I got a promotion."

"Cutting is dangerous," Quidilla said and shook his head. "You'll have to break in a whole new set of muscles."

"Mr. Davies doubled my wages."

"So you think you're rich, is that it? Why you got that other stuff?"

"The paper and pencils are for you. I'm going to teach you to write so when I'm not around you can still write to your family."

Hope lit Quidilla's face. "You can teach me to read and write?"

"Yep. First you have to learn the alphabet, then I can teach you to read."

George printed the letters on the first page of the notebook, both upper and lower case. On the second page he wrote the vowels.

Every night, Quidilla learned five new letters. During the day while they cut cane, George and Quidilla sang the *A,B,C* song George had learned in first grade. Soon the whole crew was chanting the alphabet.

Quidilla was a quick learner. In no time, he was reading words. Discarded week-old Sunday newspapers became their textbooks. For the first time since that awful night, George felt like everything was going to be okay. He almost forgot that he was a curse to his family and friends.

"That's unbelievable," Quidilla said, after he stumbled through a news article. "It can't be true. I must have read it wrong."

"You didn't," George said. "It's true. Scientists have sent a rocket into outer space just like in the movies. I wonder what Jonathan would think about it?"

"Who's Jonathan? Your brother?"

"No." Suddenly, the excitement of reading about a rocket speeding fifty miles straight up didn't seem so exciting. "Just a friend. We were in the same class at school, and he liked science stuff. He moved away in the eighth grade." Shut up, he told himself. You're babbling. Out loud he said, "Read the next headline."

"C.I.A. Formed. What is this C.I.A.?"

"I don't know. Let me look." George leaned closer. "It's the Central Intelligence Agency."

"Which means?"

George scanned the article and shook his head. "I don't really know. I think it's some kind of new police department."

"Just what we need." Quidilla laughed. "More police."

"You got that right," George said. "I think we've studied enough for today."

He went to sleep that night feeling guilty that he hadn't told Quidilla his plan to leave come payday. It never seemed to be the right time. He'd even toyed with the idea of just leaving, but that wouldn't be fair to the man who'd treated him like a son. Quidilla deserved better.

The night before payday, George realized he couldn't put it off any longer. When Quidilla came back with the newspaper, he'd tell him.

"George?" Quidilla said, holding up the newspaper so George could read the headlines. "Does this say what I think it does?"

The headlines announced in large block print, PHILIPPINES GRANTED INDEPENDENCE.

"My country is free? Read me the whole article. Don't leave out a word." He thrust the newspaper into George's hand. "Wait. Let me get everyone so they can hear, too."

George's confession would have to wait.

9

PAYDAY

George waited almost two hours before it was his turn to pick up his pay.

"*Bango Tag*," the pay clerk said.

George handed his tag to the man and waited. The man ran his finger down a row of numbers. He reached into a drawer and pulled out two quarters, one dime and three pennies.

"What's this?" George asked.

"Your pay."

"But I started at fifty cents a day, and two weeks ago Mr. Davies doubled my salary."

"Yes, the records show you were hired at the beginning of the month, worked two half days the first week and full-day weeks thereafter. Your wages were raised to a dollar an hour on the sixteenth."

"That adds up to $17.50," George said.

"Your math is good."

"Then why did you only give me sixty-three cents?"

"It shows here, you made several purchases at the company store. A machete, new shirt, and some miscellaneous items. They've been subtracted against your pay."

George clenched his fists. "The foreman sent me to get the machete, and he's the one who ripped up my shirt. He didn't tell me I had to pay for them."

The clerk smiled sympathetically. "I'm sorry for the misunderstanding, but you really don't think the mill is in the business of charity, do you?"

"Charity?" George said, trying to hold back his anger. The hours of backbreaking work didn't feel like charity. Not in the least.

"What's holding up the line?" a man yelled.

"Take your wages and move on," the clerk said. "Next month, try not to spend all your money before it's earned."

George clutched the change in an angry fist. He wanted to throw it in the paymaster's face, but that wouldn't do any good. It wasn't the man's fault. It was Mr. Davies' fault. The foreman had tricked him. George stomped out of the building muttering words that would have landed him in detention if he was still in school. His fury fueled his trek back to the Plantation Camp, kicking rocks as he went.

How would he pay for the canoe? He had to find Quidilla. Maybe he would lend George the money. As soon as he found his parents, he'd pay it back. With interest.

Quidilla had returned to camp earlier and sat in front of the tent, reading a newspaper. He looked up and smiled when he saw George.

"How does it feel to be a wage earner?"

George punched his open palm like a prize fighter who'd lost a fight.

"What's wrong?"

"What's wrong?" George asked. "I killed myself all month for a lousy sixty-three cents. It's slavery."

"It is the way of the world. Rich men get richer on the poor man's labor."

"Then poor men shouldn't do it."

"But they do, it is part of life. Some men are destined to be rich. Others poor. Even the Bible says, *the poor will always be with us*."

"That's not fair."

"Life isn't fair. Still, my coming here has allowed my sons to be educated. One day, I hope they will be among the rich men because I had the opportunity to cut sugar cane."

"You expect me to believe that cutting cane is an opportunity? That's crazy."

Quidilla chuckled. "For me, an opportunity. For you, a lesson." His face turned serious. "George, I will miss your company. You have taught me to read and write. And much about determination."

George stiffened, and he felt his face flush. His words came out in a rush. "How did you know I planned to leave? I haven't told anyone. I'm sorry I didn't tell you sooner, but it doesn't matter now. I can't leave. I don't have the money for the canoe."

"Canoe? What are you talking about?" Quidilla looked puzzled. "I was trying to tell you that I've booked a passage on a ship to the Philippines. I leave tomorrow night. I'm going home to my family. You should do the same."

"Great," George said, feeling suddenly empty. What was he going to do now? He couldn't ask Quidilla for a loan. He'd have to work another month, but it would be lonely without his friend.

"You should leave, too. If you stay, the company will own you, taking your wages faster than you can earn them. Go home to your family. You know they're waiting for you to come."

"I don't know," George said truthfully. He wasn't sure how his parents felt about him. Maybe once they'd learned about how he'd cursed Kapuna and Tutu, they wouldn't want anything to do with him. And what about the man in the field? The one George replaced. Had it been an accident? Or part of his curse?

"Go now," Quidilla urged. "You said it yourself. It's slavery. You don't belong here. Don't fall into their trap. Go while you can, before you're in debt to the mill."

What Quidilla said made sense. Even if George wasn't sure how to find his parents. Or if they were still on Molokai. It was time to leave. Even if his parents didn't want him, he couldn't stay.

"Thank you, Quidilla. You have been like a father to me."

"And you to me, a son."

"Say goodbye to the others for me."

They embraced.

George got his things and headed across a field in the direction of the tattooed woman's shed. He didn't know if the machete and the seventy-three cents would buy the canoe, but he couldn't wait any longer. Maybe she'd listen if he explained how he'd earned the money, but had it taken from him.

When George arrived at the shed, it looked deserted. The woman was nowhere in sight. He tried the door; it was locked. He peeked inside. It was empty except for cobwebs and dust. It looked like no one had ever lived there. But then he saw the woman's carved walking stick leaned in a corner. Had something happened to her?

Three of the large canoes were gone, but the smaller canoe rested in the sand. It'd been oiled and smelled of coconuts, readied for the sea. In the prow was a sturdy stick wrapped with a coil of fishing line. Next to it was a woven fan with at least a dozen fish hooks.

Should he wait for her to return? Would she come back? George wasn't sure, but a burning desire to leave overcame him. He couldn't wait. He'd pay for the canoe with what he had. The machete was worth more than the ten dollars he'd promised her. Besides, she must have been expecting him. The canoe was readied for a long trip. She was probably just gone for the day, but who knew when she'd come back? He couldn't wait all day.

Ceremoniously he placed his machete, the sixty-three cents, his shirt, and the *Bango Tag* on the threshold of the shed.

"Thank you," he said, feeling the breeze on his face.

Now he had nothing. Not even a penny to buy food.

He pulled the canoe down the beach. Looking back, he thought he saw the door of the shed open. He blinked and looked again. The door was closed. It must have been a trick of the sun and shade. Or was it? The machete and shirt were gone. A chill ran down his spine. He'd swear she hadn't been in the shed when he looked.

His mind must be playing tricks on him.

He shoved the boat into the water and jumped aboard. He'd paddle close to the shore until he came to the place where Molokai looked the closest before he struck out into open water. If he remembered right, it was only eight miles between the two islands.

He sailed north, careful to steer clear of reefs. Around noon, he paddled into a small horseshoe-shaped bay pushed into the island. It was surrounded by craggy lava and lush green vegetation.

It would be a good place to rest before he headed across the strait.

10

OPEN WATER

The small bay was calm like an inland pond. Its narrow entrance blocked the rough surf, leaving only soft waves to lap up against the canoe. It was the perfect place to catch lunch and take a break, thought George. He was close. In just a couple of days he should find his parents.

He jumped into the water and pulled the canoe onto the rocky beach. Mini lava boulders covered the ground like giant sand grains. Gingerly, he climbed over the water-worn rocks to a bush. He stripped a few leaves and flowers from a branch and returned to the boat.

Quidilla had taught him well. In a few minutes he'd fashioned a realistic-looking insect from the leaves and slipped it onto a fishhook. It might not work as well as live bait, but it'd do. George tied the lure onto the fishing line and plopped it into the water, jerking the line up and down like the insect was alive.

To his surprise, almost immediately something hit and dragged the line. George spun the stick, wrapping the line as he went, and pulled in a small perch. It wasn't big enough to eat, but it would make good bait.

Twenty minutes later, George was on the beach roasting an Uhu over a fire. It didn't take long to cook the fish. It was good. He ate slow, savoring every bite and thinking about his trip across open water. Should he wait until the next morning and give himself the whole day to make the crossing? It shouldn't take all that long. It was only eight miles. Judging from the position of the sun, it was still early afternoon. Plenty of daylight left before sunset. That decided it.

Once he was out of the small bay, he paddled toward the dark distant shoreline of Molokai. The winds had picked up, and the open sea was choppy. It took more energy to keep the canoe on course. Still he paddled with ease. The tattooed woman had been right. The cane work had made him stronger. Looking back, he smiled. There was a lot of sea between him and Maui. Looking forward, he frowned.

He should be closer to Molokai, but the island seemed even farther away than when he'd started. A cold realization wormed its way into his thoughts, and he shivered. The tides were dragging him northeast instead of northwest. Away from both islands and into open sea. He fought the current and paddled like his life depended on it. It did. If he didn't get to land, no one would ever find him stranded somewhere in the middle of the Pacific.

His muscles burned, but he wouldn't give up. He couldn't. Every dip of the paddle went deeper and he pulled harder. Turning the boat east, he tried to paddle across the current like when caught in a rip tide. It didn't work. Land drifted farther and farther away. where was the tide taking him?

The night sky grew dark, and then was brightened by the moon. Silvery waves crested around him. He rested, his lips parched. It was crazy. He was surrounded by water and dying of thirst. Taking a few deep breaths through his nose, he started to paddle even though he wasn't even sure of his direction any more.

At some point he passed out from sheer exhaustion. He jolted awake to the first light of a new day and swiped crusty sleep from his eyes. Where was he? Then he remembered. Panic raced down his chest and his heart pounded in his throat. Was he halfway to China?

The wind had quieted and the sea seemed calm. Luckily the paddle was still in the boat. He grabbed it and maneuvered the canoe into a three-sixty-degree turn. By some miracle he spotted the shadow outlines of two islands to the southeast. Land!

He whooped, recognizing Maui and Molokai. He still had a chance. Molokai looked the closest. He started paddling with a renewed energy. He wouldn't relax until he stood on solid ground. The sky lightened, and he was surprised at his incredible speed. The current was with him instead of against him. In record time he was there, right on the tip of the island.

What a beautiful morning.

He paddled hard and caught a wave. The boat thrust ahead as it surged forward toward a valley nestled between sharp, steep mountains.

"Woooo hooooo!" shouted George, holding the paddle over his head as he rode the wave toward the sandy beach. It felt like he was flying, but then something strange happened. The wave didn't stop when it reached the beach. It couldn't, it was too high. In an instant, George knew something was wrong. He braced himself.

The wave surged high over the beach and kept going inland. To his right, a house swept off its pilings, its roof tossed into the air like a kite. It splashed down close, tipping the canoe and drenching George with a huge spray.

Flooding the valley, the water thrust George on a destructive path. He struggled to to stay upright in the canoe. The sea water churned up tended taro fields, destroying buildings and flattening trees. The wave lost its momentum and slowed, the water level dropping as it began to pull the canoe back toward the sea.

George paddled hard, fighting against the reverse surge. He couldn't let it pull him back out to the ocean. Not now. But the sea's drag on the canoe was too strong to fight. He jumped, landing in water up to his waist. The current pulled him off balance. He managed to spin in the water and regained his footing, but the power of the receding water was relentless. It tugged at his shorts and pulled them down around his ankles. He stumbled out of the water like a hobbled cow.

He slipped on the wet grass, and his fingers landed on something soft and squishy. He snatched his hand back and stared open-mouthed. It was an octopus. Right here in the grass. He scrambled to his feet, pulled up his wet pants and stared at the receding ocean.

The dirty sea water sucked back out as quickly as it had come in. Debris was scattered across the field like it was World War III and the Japanese had dropped another bomb. Fish flopped for air. Eels. Octopus. Stuff was strewn everywhere. Part of a roof. A pickup turned on its side, water gushing from the window. Parts of buildings were now heaps of wood. Beyond the fields, the sea kept retreating. Curls of the lava reef were exposed in the sparkling sunshine. It looked like someone had pulled the plug in a bathtub.

He stood in the remnant of what must have been a taro field. It was a large valley, bowl-shaped like a giant amphitheater. A river flowed down its center and emptied into the sea. In the far distance, he could see a waterfall cascading down a steep cliff.

What could have made the sea do this, he wondered. Then it hit George. It was a huge tidal wave. He remembered studying about them in fifth grade. Whoa! He'd ridden a tidal wave and hadn't even realized it.

Shoot. If he remembered right, tidal waves came in a series. Sometimes four waves, or as many as seven. Going out and then coming back harder, higher. Had he ridden the first or the last wave in the series?

He tried to picture Mrs. Osaka at the front of the classroom. It was one of the days he'd really listened. Tidal waves, unlike arithmetic or flower germination, were fascinating. In his mind he heard her voice. *The interval between waves can be five minutes or forty minutes. It all depends on how far away the earthquake is that caused them.*

How much time did he have? Twenty minutes? Ten?

He needed to get to higher ground.

11

HALAWA VALLEY

George spotted a road zigzagging up the steep hillside. He ran toward where he thought the road must begin its climb between the "V" where two hills met. He plunged through knee-deep grass and pushed through a thicket of low undergrowth.

Yes! He'd guessed right. On the other side, a dirt road wandered along the river's edge up the valley. It was easier running, and he lengthened his stride. He had to reach high ground before the next wave struck. Although the first wave hadn't come this far inland, a second or third one could. He had to keep going.

A stitch of pain worked its way under his ribs, and he pressed his elbow to his side. He zoomed past houses along the road, but they looked deserted. He rounded another turn. Thank goodness. Just two football field lengths stood between him and where the road began its climb up the mountain.

His relief was short-lived. The roar of the ocean grew louder. Oh no. The next tidal wave must have arrived. He pulled one last ounce of energy from his fear and ran faster past the last house on the right. That's when he heard someone calling for help.

"Let me out of here!" a girl's voice cried from behind a weather faded green-house near to the road. Her shouts were accompanied by a pounding noise. "This isn't funny anymore."

"Where are you?" George yelled.

"Over here," the voice called from a large chicken coop to the side of the house. "The door's stuck. I can't get out."

He dashed to the shed, looking over his shoulder. A frothy ten-foot wall of water churned up the road. It was traveling at an alarming speed.

"Hurry," she called. "It stinks in here."

Someone had barred the door from the outside. He popped the two-by-four piece of lumber from its slot and the door flew open. A wild-eyed girl close to his age rushed out in a flock of shrieking chickens. Her dark eyes burned with anger, announcing that she wanted to kill somebody.

"I'm going to stuff poi up his nose and fill his bed with cockroaches," she screamed. Her heart-shaped lips frowned.

George grabbed her arm. "Come on, we have to get to high ground."

She jerked away, transferring her anger to George. "I don't know who you are. I'm not going anywhere with you."

"Then don't," George said, looking past her. His eyes popped open. "But you'd better run. The wave's almost here."

He ran.

She must have caught the urgency in his voice and turned. "Yikes!" She started after him. "What about the chickens?"

"They can fly."

They ran hard, but George was winded. He slowed. The girl caught up and grabbed his arm as she passed him. The wave chased them up the lower portion of the road and stopped. It began to recede, dragging the chicken coop toward the sea. They watched it in horror as it smashed up against a tree and splintered. If George hadn't come along, she would have been inside.

"You saved my life," the girl said. "Who are you?"

George leaned over, his hands on his knees, and gasped for breath. "I'm George."

"Well, George, I don't know where you came from, but I think the *spirits* must have sent you or I'd be shark bait." Now that she was't glaring at him, she seemed nice.

He laughed, looking at her and thinking how pretty she was when she smiled. Looking at him like he was some kind of a hero. "The *spirits* didn't send me. I was fishing in my canoe and got caught by the wave."

He couldn't tell her he was on the run from authorities in Maui, had taken a canoe, and was searching for his parents.

"What's your name?" he asked.

From up the hill, they were interrupted by voices raised in panic, "Claire! Claire!"

"I'm here," the girl shouted and started up the road, motioning for George to follow. She ran like a light-footed deer, her hair flying behind her. She was pretty, not pretty like Jonathan's sister Alice, but pretty because of how she had looked at him. George felt his face grow warm.

"It's my family," she said and then shouted, "I'm all right. I'm coming."

A man rounded a bend, running down the hill like a locomotive. Claire raced to him.

He picked her up and swept her into a hug.

"Thank the stars you're okay," he said.

"I wouldn't be, if George hadn't come along. Someone locked me in the chicken house."

"Why would someone do that?"

The rest of Claire's family and neighbors appeared. A boy who looked four or five hung back. When he saw Claire, tears welled in his eyes. He ran to her, buried his head in her side and blurted out, "It was just an April Fool's joke. Like when Uncle Jonus called and said there was an earthquake in Alaska and that there was going to be a tidal wave. I thought it was a joke. He's always joking. I didn't know the tidal wave was for real."

Claire's father's face was dark with fury. "It's a good thing this boy came along." He held out his hand. "We owe you a big thanks."

George shook the hard and firm farmer's hand.

"I don't want to think of what would have happened if you hadn't come along," the man said. "Where did you come from?"

George repeated his story that he'd been fishing and caught in the tidal wave.

"Your parents will be worried," Claire's father said. "We'll try to contact them as soon as possible."

George shook his head, "You don't have to. My parents were killed at Pearl Harbor. I lived in an orphanage until I was old enough to take care of myself. The only thing I have to remember them by is this necklace," he said and fingered the white turtle carving that hung from his neck. "Now I'm on my own."

This last lie sent a chill down George's back. What if it was true? What if he really was an orphan? What if when he found his parents, they didn't want him? And never had.

"Stay with us as long as you like," Claire's father said. "Tonight we'll *talk story*."

George gulped. He'd have to think up something believable.

12

TALK STORY

George sat alone in the shadow, out of the flickering light of the campfire—his arms crossed, and trying to look invisible. Claire squatted down next to him.

"What are you doing over here?" she asked.

He shrugged.

She pointed to the men, women, and children seated where her house had stood before the second wave hit. "You can't sit over here. You have to join us. Everyone is looking forward to hearing you *talk story*."

George's stomach felt like Pele had poured hot lava into it. He did not want to *talk story* in front of a bunch of strangers. It was bad enough having to tell lies to Claire and her family. Especially when his curse had destroyed their home.

Claire dragged him to his feet, pulled him to an empty space on a log, and pushed him onto it. She plopped down next to him. The campfire flames leaped into the air, casting flickers of yellow shadows across the tired yet hopeful faces. It was time to *talk story*.

"George," Claire's father said. "You want to be first?"

"That's okay," George stammered. "Someone else can start."

A round-faced woman in a red flowered muumuu stood. "I've never liked April Fool's Day and most of you know why," she said and winked. Several people laughed as she sat.

That was short, thought George. Could he get away with just one sentence?

The next man talked longer, and George realized that one sentence would not be enough.

Claire's father was the last adult to speak. "Lanikaula's magic is still powerful."

George leaned over and whispered to Claire, "Who's Lanikaula?"

She put her finger to her lips.

"He brought George to save our Claire. Thank you."

Heads nodded and turned to stare at George. His face reddened. They expected him to speak next, but to his relief, Claire bounced to her feet.

"We've all heard the stories of Lanikaula since we could talk, but George hasn't." She smiled at him. "Lanikaula was the most powerful sorcerer in all Hawaii and my ancestor. He was feared. Other sorcerers grew jealous of his great magic and plotted against him." She went on to tell of how he was tricked and killed by a rival and then buried in a sacred grove of kukui. "His spirit still lives there. And now, it's your turn, George."

"It's late. My story can wait."

"It's not late," Claire said. "And even if it were, we'd want to hear your story."

"We insist," Claire's father added.

"Okay," George said. He stared at the treetops, afraid to look at his audience. "I am the first son of my father, the first son of his father, and was given to my grandparents to bring joy and hope to them in their old age. We all lived together, and when I was old enough, it became my job to fish for my family."

He paused and lowered his eyes. To his surprise, everyone looked interested. They were buying his story. Hey, maybe he could do this.

"Because I always caught lots of fish, I was hired by a restaurant. It's a great job. I get paid to do what I love. To fish all day."

George's was the last story. It was late and everyone headed back to where they'd set up temporary camps. He'd been invited to stay with Claire's family for the night. He accepted. Long after everyone had gone to sleep, he lay awake on the ground, staring at the stars. Thinking of his curse. His fingers stroked his father's necklace. Hoping his parents would be happy to see him.

What would Claire's family think if he'd told them the truth? Would they still treat him like family if they knew he cursed everyone he got close to? Would they still think him brave, if they knew his best friend was a leper?

Would they still think him a hero, if they thought George might be a leper, too? Probably not. He couldn't tell them. Instead, he'd stay for just a few days, help with the cleanup, and learn all he could about Molokai.

After breakfast the next morning, Claire's father said, "George and Claire, you're on chicken detail. Round up as many as you can find."

"How will we know which hens are ours?" Claire asked.

"Doesn't matter," he said. "We can worry about that later."

George and Claire found the roof of the chicken house, or what was left of it. It was propped on the trunk of a palm tree forty feet from where it had been before the tidal wave hit.

They looked at each other. George knew they were thinking the same thing. What if she hadn't got out?

"You saved my life," Claire said.

George's face colored. "Anyone would have done it. Besides, it was your loud mouth that saved you," he said, trying to change the subject.

"Think you're funny? Guess again." She took a swipe at him with her fist.

George ducked. "Hey, I won't be able to work if you break my arm."

She rolled her eyes and glared at him. "So, where's the rest of the coop?"

George pointed. "I'd say it is there, there, and there."

This time she laughed.

"It looks like the chicken wire fence is still here," George said. "It's just bent and mangled in a few places. We can fix it."

Chasing chickens turned out to be easy. By the time Claire and George had the fence rebuilt, about twenty chickens had gathered to scratch in the damp ground for bugs.

"Don't tell them the chicken food is gone," whispered Claire. "Or we'll never get them in the pen."

George laughed.

They shooed the chickens inside and wired the gate shut.

Claire started pulling up grass and throwing it into the pen.

"What are you doing?" George asked.

"We have to give them something to eat or they'll feel betrayed. Make yourself useful. Find something for a water dish."

"What now?" George asked, once the chickens were watered and fed.

"I guess we should find my father."

They rechecked the pen and headed toward the beach.

"So," she said, staring at the sky, her voice almost a whisper, "George, do you have a girlfriend?"

George's ears reddened. "No. Why do you ask?"

"Just wondering."

"Oh."

She smiled and laughed. "Aren't you going to ask me?"

"Ask you what?"

Claire looked him in the eye. "Aren't you going to ask me if I have a boyfriend?"

His uncertainty slammed him again. Would she still like him if she knew his best friend was a leper? And maybe he might be one, too? She wouldn't even want to be his friend.

"So, ask me!"

"Do you?"

"No," she said and reached for his hand. Her hand was warm and sticky, but not as hot as his face felt. A long time ago he'd imagined what it'd be like holding hands with Jonathan's cousin Alice, but it was nothing like this. This felt real. Nice.

"Look, there's your dad."

Claire dropped his hand.

Claire's father spotted them at the same time. He waved them over.

"Operation chicken, complete," George said and saluted.

"What next?" Claire asked.

"Your mother needs your help. George, you can help salvage. Everything we find, we're putting over there." He pointed to a rock terrace half full of sodden treasures.

"Where do you want me to start?"

Claire's father held out his arms and gestured to the whole valley. "Take your choice."

George headed to the river. Most things he saw weren't worth picking up. Then he spotted a radio half buried in mud. He dug it out, twisted the dial, and to his amazement, music blared.

The radio announcer broke in, "A seven-point earthquake in Alaska set in motion the tidal waves that rocked the Hawaiian Islands. The series of disastrous tidal waves that struck Hawaii yesterday morning was no April Fool's Day joke. One hundred seventy lives were lost, and millions of dollars in damage reported."

George switched off the radio. He stared at the sky and suddenly felt free. His curse couldn't have caused the tidal wave. It just happened. Not because of him, but because of some earthquake three thousand miles away. A tingle raised the hair at the top of his head. A shiver ran down his spine. He whooped. He was free. He wasn't a curse to everyone he loved.

Mr. Kim was wrong.

Did this mean that meant he didn't have to lie anymore? He could tell Claire and her family the truth.

Or should he?

After telling them so many lies, it would be awkward. Maybe he should just leave without telling them. He shook his head and gritted his teeth. No, that wouldn't be right. They deserved the truth. Even in the midst of disaster, they'd treated him like *ohana*. Like he belonged. He'd just have to wait for the right moment.

Maybe they could help him find his parents.

"Yes!" he shouted. A flock of seabirds abandoned their scavenging and took flight. He chased after them and ran up the beach with the radio clutched to his chest.

Near the pile of salvaged goods, Robert, Claire's little brother, was drawing in the sand with a stick. When he saw George, he jumped up and down. "You found our radio," Robert shouted.

"And it still works." George turned it on. Swing music blasted from the box.

The two of them jumped around like they were dancing on hot coals. They didn't notice Claire's father until the music abruptly stopped.

"Don't waste the batteries," he said. "Robert, take George for a dip in the pool."

Robert's eyes grew large and he grinned. "Come on, George. We can swim and take a shower at the same time."

"Where?" George asked.

Robert pointed to the distant waterfall cascading between cliffs. "It's fun. First, I'll be a little fishy and you can catch me. Then I'll be a big shark and bite your toes."

George laughed and followed the little boy.

13

BAD MALE

Lunch was fish roasted over an open fire. Claire and her mother took the dishes to the stream to wash.

Two days had passed since finding the radio, and George still hadn't found the courage to tell Claire's father the truth. It was now or never. If he waited any longer, he'd never tell them, and they'd never understand why he left them. Especially not Claire. She wasn't as pretty as Jonathan's cousin Alice, but she was nice and the first girl he'd liked as a friend.

"Time to get back to work," Claire's father said. Robert jumped up and started for the beach.

George stood, but didn't follow. He took a big breath, held it a moment and blurted out, "Wait. I have something to tell you, sir."

"Call me Tono. You've earned the right." Claire's father smiled. "I thought you might. The last couple of days you've looked like you were carrying a secret."

"I didn't come to Molokai by accident."

The man's eyebrows raised.

"I wasn't out fishing when I was caught by the tidal wave."

"You're a runaway?"

"No, I came to find my parents."

George fished in his pocket and pulled out the crumpled envelope with the clipped corner.

"This is a letter from my father. It's all I have."

Tono took the envelope. He squinted to read the smudged return address. "St. Francis," he whispered, and his smile deserted his face. The envelope dropped to the ground.

He took a step back from George. "Show me your leg."

"My leg?"

How had Tono found out about the white patch on his leg? And then he remembered his swim under the waterfall. Robert must have said something.

"It's nothing. Just a scar." George swallowed. "I burned myself."

"Show me your leg."

George pulled up the leg of his shorts. The white patch seemed lighter than it had and maybe a little bigger.

Claire's father's face blanched. "You have to leave and never come back."

"Why?"

"St. Francis is on Kalaupapa. The place of dead men walking." Dark storm clouds gathered and cast an ominous shadow over the valley. "It's the leper colony."

"What?" George said as his lunch churned. "I don't believe you. My father works on a sugar plantation."

"Where?"

"At the mill on the west end of the island."

"It closed fifteen years ago. No one lives in Kalaupapa but nuns, priests, doctors and lepers. Is your father a doctor?"

George said nothing.

"The disease runs in families," Tono said.

The burning in George's stomach erupted into a sharp pain. "I don't have it. Tutu and Kapuna didn't have it. My parents aren't lepers."

"You were probably born in Kalaupapa. Babies are sent away unless they have the disease."

George felt numb. All these years Kapuna and Tutu had lied to him. Lied about his parents. Lied about why he lived with them. What about his sister? Had they lied about her, too? Was she a leper?

What else had they lied about?

George dry swallowed. "I'll go."

"I'm sorry about your family," Tono said. "But I have to think about the safety of mine. I'll tell Claire goodbye for you."

George reached out to shake the man's hand. The man didn't return the gesture. Instead he took another step back and pointed to the road. "It's a full day's walk to the next town, and half the day's already gone. There's a ranch at the top. Maybe they'll let you sleep in their barn."

George's throat felt like an invisible hand had gripped it and squeezed. Once again, he felt totally alone.

"I understand," George said. He reached down, picked up his parent's letter and started up the road. Alone again.

He bit his lip and willed himself to move. Unblinking, he stared at his feet as they shuffled forward like Frankenstein's monster. He didn't notice the breeze on his face or hear the call of a uau kani bird in the distance.

Someone grabbed his arm and pulled him back into the present.

"George!"

He turned.

It was Claire. Her face was flushed and she was breathing hard from running to catch up.

She released his arm and put her hands on her hips. "How could you leave without saying goodbye? I thought you liked me."

"I do."

"Then why are you leaving?"

"I don't belong here."

"Did my father send you away?"

"It's not his fault, Claire. I might be sick."

"What do you mean?"

He paused, trying to hold onto the moment before he had to see the look of horror on her face. In a whisper, he said, "My parents are lepers."

Saying it somehow made it true. The hair on his neck bristled, sending a shiver down his spine.

"That's ridiculous," Claire said.

"Your father said it runs in families. I have to leave. I have to find my parents."

"What if they don't want to see you?" She looked away and kicked at the ground. "I mean, what if they don't want you to see them?"

George shrugged. "Maybe they won't, but I have to go anyway."

"But you might catch it. Aren't you afraid?"

"I don't know."

"I'm going with you," she said.

"No! You can't come with me."

"Why not?"

"Because you belong here and I belong . . ." He let the words trail off. He didn't know where he belonged. "Hey, I just don't want you to come. I don't want you to get sick."

A warm raindrop struck his face.

Claire took his hand, leaned in, and her lips brushed his. She stepped back. "George, you won't forget me?"

George tried to smile. Suddenly, saying goodbye to Claire hit him. Would he ever see her again?

"I'll never forget you, Claire. I promise. Not ever. Goodbye."

"Bye, George." A tear trickled down her cheek.

"Claire!" Her father's angry voice called from down the hill.

"I'd better go. Stay on this road until you get to Kaunakakai. There you go north to the trail-head that leads down to Kalaupapa. Except for a boat, it's the only way in."

"Thanks."

Claire turned and raced down the road. Before she reached the turn, she stopped to wave one last time and then disappeared.

George continued his climb up the steep twisted road. The jungle canopy gave way to tall trees and open grassy fields. As he walked, his mind traveled in endless circles.

If his parents lived in Kalaupapa, maybe that's where he belonged, too.

In his heart he knew it was probably only a matter of time before the leprosy claimed him like it had Jonathan. Maybe the patch of white skin from the burn wasn't a scar, but the first stages of leprosy.

At least then he'd belong somewhere.

14

THE ROAD

George heard the whine of a truck's engine. A battered blue pickup roared past, dragging blue smoke behind its wheels. He leaped into the ditch, his feet sinking into mud from last night's rain. It was the first vehicle on the road that morning.

The pickup slid sideways and stopped. The front door opened. George couldn't see who was driving, but the man's words were welcome.

"Need a ride? Hop in."

George ran to the passenger side, opened the door, and stared. The driver was the strangest person he'd ever seen. Not a Hawaiian, but an old white guy in a pair of grimy shorts, ragged at the cuffs. His gray hair was matted into long hair-ball ropes. A mongoose skull swung from the rearview mirror, and a chicken perched on the seat back near the man's shoulder. White chicken droppings stained the upholstery.

The huge red hen squawked, flapped her wings, and launched herself at George.

"Grab Red, don't let her out of the cab," the man ordered.

Instinctively, George grabbed the hen like a line-ball hit and tossed her back into the cab.

"Good hands," the man said and laughed as he grabbed his chicken. "Jump in and get the door shut before she can try it again."

George hopped onto the seat, but almost slipped out again when his feet hit the hay on the floor.

"Don't step on the eggs. Red wouldn't like it," the man said and held out his hand to George. "Hi, I'm Larry Lee. You've already met Red. We own this here island. I'm sure you've heard of me. I am the White Kahuna of Molokai!"

The cab of the truck reeked of chicken manure mixed with ten-year-old sweat and grime.

George tried to breathe through his mouth as his stomach roiled.

"What's your name, boy?"

"George."

Larry Lee stomped on the gas pedal and the pickup shot forward.

"I've been expecting an apprentice, but I didn't expect a George. It doesn't seem right. I think I'll call you Coconut Boy. You like that?"

George didn't have to answer because Larry Lee kept on talking.

"I've needed an apprentice for a long time. Someone to train in my special brand of kahuna sorcery. Someone to hunt the mongoose that's stealing my magic. And someone to do my dishes."

George frowned. What kind of nut was this guy?

Larry Lee let go of the steering wheel. As he did, the pickup swerved and bumped in and out of the ditch. It barreled driverless as he pointed to his head with both index fingers.

"I have a lot of knowledge in this noggin to pass on."

George braced himself and reached for the steering wheel.

Larry Lee batted George's hand away, grabbed the steering wheel, and gunned the accelerator. Miraculously, the truck was still on the road.

"You don't know how lucky you are, Coconut Boy."

"Yeah," George said, hoping he'd get out of the truck alive. "Could you pull over? I think we passed my stop."

Larry Lee threw back his head and laughed. "If I did that, how would I train you? Who would cook my meals? No, Coconut Boy, your training starts this second. From now on you'll do exactly what Red or I tell you. Got that?"

The chicken chose that moment to jump onto George's shoulder.

"Lesson one, you say–" Larry Lee's blue eye's became slits in a stony face. "Yes, mighty kahuna, all-powerful one."

Red pecked George's cheek.

George shouted, "Stop the truck and let me out!"

Larry Lee laughed maniacally and shook his head. His ropy hair flew about his head like angry snakes.

George clung to the passenger door as the pickup careened around corners, sliding close to the edge of steep cliffs that dropped off into the thick jungle.

The truck barreled down the road toward the ocean. There was only one thing to do. If George was going to live, he'd have to jump.

When the man slowed for a hairpin curve, George threw open the door and leaped from the truck. He hit the ground hard, rolling in mud.

The pickup traveled another forty feet and screeched to a stop. Its gears ground in protest. Larry Lee started backing up.

George bolted into the brush. Scrabbling on his hands and knees, he half slid, half ran down toward the ocean below.

The pickup's engine shut off. A door opened and slammed shut.

George scrambled faster. He had to get down to the water. If the crazy man caught up, George would have to swim.

"You can run, but you can't hide, Coconut Boy," Larry Lee shouted from the road.

Panting, George crouched under a bush and hoped the man would just leave.

"I've captured your *mojo*! I hold your spirit in my hand."

George didn't move. What was Larry Lee babbling about now?

"You may think you've escaped, but I promise, you will return to serve me. I have your Turtle."

George's hand flew to his neck. His father's necklace was gone. No. How had Larry Lee gotten it? He clenched his teeth and punched his thigh.

Larry Lee let out a Tarzan yell.

Something hit George in the back of the head and clattered below. Was Larry Lee throwing rocks at him? George peered down at the missile and saw that it was an empty tin can. It'd come to rest some twenty feet below him on a narrow trail that hugged the steep cliff.

The pickup door slammed and its engine hummed to life. Larry Lee, Red, and the rattletrap pickup continued their death plunge down the steep hillside.

George let out a burst of air and leaned back to catch his breath. He wiped sweat from his brow. It was hot and he was dying of thirst. And he was angry. The crazy man had taken the one thing that connected him to his parents. Now he had nothing to prove he was their son.

He climbed down to the trail. It'd be harder walking than the road, but at least he wouldn't run into Larry Lee. The track grew wider as it curled around the point. He needed to find some water soon. His mouth was as dry as he imagined the desert, his lips sore and his tongue thick. Then he saw it and grinned. Fresh water!

In the elbow of a small inlet, a rocky stream emptied onto a tiny white sand beach.

George hurried down the slope. Waves splashed against the rocks. He paused to savor the cool mist on his hot skin. Then he saw the fishing boat. It looked like it had been flung onto the lava shelf and split in two. Half of it still whole. The other half splintered from the force of an angry sea.

How long had it been there? Not too long. Its red and blue paint still looked bright and fresh. Had the boat been caught in the tidal wave?

He scanned the wreckage. There was a lot of stuff near what was left of the bow. Pillows, boxes and . . . George stared open-mouthed.

It was a man. A man who wasn't moving. Except for in the movies, George had never seen a dead person. He shivered.

"Hey, mister? You okay?" he called.

It was a dumb question. Even if the man was alive, it was obvious he wasn't okay.

George moved closer, watching the man's chest to see if it moved. It was too hard to tell. Steeling himself for the worst, George clenched his jaws and went to the man's side.

The white man wore a dark business suit with a green tie. His hair was carrot red, and he had a small goatee. He didn't look dead, just asleep.

"Hey, are you alive?"

George thought he saw the man's right thumb move. Or was that his imagination? He squatted and touched the man's hand. It was hot, like it was on fire.

George shook the man's shoulder. "Hey, mister, wake up."

The man's eyes flew open.

15

FEVER TALK

A shadow of pain crossed the man's face. His eyes closed and he mumbled something in a voice so faint, George couldn't understand. The man started coughing.

"Mister, you're going to be okay," George said and loosened the man's tie. "I'll get help."

The man's eyes opened again. He grabbed George's arm and muttered more unintelligible words.

"I don't understand," George said. "You want water?"

The man's eyes grew frantic. His fingers tightened like a vise, pinching George's arm. "Leather case! Brown leather case!"

George stood and looked around. "I don't see a brown leather bag."

"Find it," the man gasped.

"I will, but first you need shade."

"No, find the bag first." The man's voice was hoarse, but it carried the urgency of someone used to giving orders.

George ignored the command.

"You're burning up. I have to move you."

He lifted the man easily. The work in the sugar cane had given

George strong muscles. He carried the man to the shade of a wild guava tree.

Leaving the man propped against a rock, George returned to the stream. He dropped to his knees and gulped water. Quenching his thirst seemed to kick his mind into gear. He'd need something to carry water in, but where would he find something in the middle of nowhere? Then one of Kapuna's sayings came back to him, *one man's garbage can be another man's treasure.*

The tin can Larry Lee had thrown at him was just up the trail, just minutes away. It'd make a perfect cup. George rinsed the can, filled it and sprinted back.

Supporting the injured man's head, George tipped the water into his mouth. The water seemed to revitalize him. He grabbed the can with both hands and drank greedily.

"Don't drink too fast," George said, his own stomach feeling a little queasy. "It might make you sick."

The man lowered the can and said, "You're right. I'm a doctor. I should know better."

"A doctor? Then tell me how to help you."

The man made a poor attempt to smile. "I need you to find my doctor's bag. It's about this size." The man used his hands to show the bag was one football wide and three footballs end-to-end long. "It was in the front cabin. I think that part of the boat is still there."

"What about the other people on the boat?"

The man shook his head. His hand moved to cover his eyes. "They're gone. When the boat smashed in two, I was the only one up front." He was silent for a moment. His mouth grim. "The captain. He was a good man. He and his crew members were swallowed into the sea, along with the back of the boat."

"Oh," George said, feeling stupid. He didn't know what to say. The beach was a jumble of debris from the tidal wave, a huge mess. Just like Halawa Valley. "I'll try to find it."

"It should still be in the boat."

Walking into half a boat felt strange. Like maybe he shouldn't be in there. Not because it was unsafe, but because people had died there.

He shivered and tried the door to the stateroom. It was stuck. He kicked it open.

"Wow," he said and whistled. Even though everything was one big jumbled mess, it was one expensive boat. It must have cost a fortune. The furniture was even fancier than the furniture in Jonathan's auntie Mary's house, and she was the richest person George knew.

"If this is how doctors travel, I think I should become a doctor," he said. Somehow, talking out loud made him feel a little less nervous. "The sooner I find it, the sooner I can get out of here."

He set to work tossing things aside in search of the bag. He found three, but only one the right size. What was so important about the bag that the man cared more about it than his own life? It couldn't hurt to take a peek. The bag was locked. That settled it. The bag must be full of money.

Putting the small bag under his arm, he grabbed the two larger suitcases and carried them from the wreck.

"I've got it!" George shouted. "I found the bag and a couple more."

The man smiled. "Good job. What is your name?"

"George."

"Good solid name. You can call me Doc. Bring me the smallest case."

George sat the case next to the man.

Doc fumbled at his neck and pulled out a key on a chain. He tried, but was too weak to pull the chain over his head.

"Help me with this? I need to check that the contents are safe. You'll have to open it."

George took the key. He was excited, expecting to see a pile of money. More money than he could even imagine. He slid the key into the lock. Turned it and opened the case.

What a disappointment. There wasn't any money. No gold or anything. Just a bunch of glass medicine bottles.

"Good, they're safe," Doc said and settled back. He coughed and wiped his mouth with the back of his hand. A streak of blood stained his freckled skin.

"Doc, I need to go for help."

"First, promise me something."

"What?"

"If I don't make it, see that this medicine gets to Kalaupapa." He started to shake and cough. His face turned a grayish white in spite of the heat. "These are sulphone drugs. We've been testing them at the Carville Leprosarium in Louisiana. They stop leprosy. Promise me. You'll see they get there."

"I will," George said and crossed his fingers. Hopefully the drugs worked. If what Doc said was true, Jonathan could get well and move back home. "Now I better go."

"Wait." Doc hacked up more blood. "I have to tell you the dosage and how they're supposed to be administered."

Doc made George repeat the information three times.

"I'll be back soon," George said.

He raced to the road and ran west. He pounded on the door of the first house he came to.

A man came out. He looked like a farmer. "What do you want?"

"A man's hurt on the point. The tidal wave wrecked his boat. He needs help."

"Where exactly is the man?"

George pointed and said, "He's off the road, near that outcropping of lava."

"Then we'll need another couple of hands," the man said. "Wait here."

The man went to the house next door. When he returned he motioned for George to get in his car. The man backed out of his driveway and parked at the side of the road.

"You're not from around here, are you?" the man asked.

"No," George said, wondering why they were just sitting there. Doc needed help.

"Where did you come from? Were you on the boat?"

"You don't seem to understand," George said. "This man is hurt bad. He needs help. What are we waiting for?"

At that moment another truck with two men in it pulled up behind them. The car driver pulled onto the road. The truck followed. They raced to the spot and George led the three men to where he'd left Doc.

Doc wasn't under the tree.

"I thought you said he was in the shade," the truck driver said.

"He was when I left. He must have become confused and crawled out."

"Boy, have you led us on some sort of a goose chase?"

"No, he was hurt bad."

"He's over here," the car driver said. "Someone laid him on his back and crossed his wrists over his heart. He's dead."

"That's odd," the truck driver said. "Why would someone stick a red chicken feather in each hand?"

George didn't want to look into Doc's dead face, but he had to. He grabbed the feathers and threw them into the wind. They fluttered into the sea and disappeared in a frothy wave. Kneeling at Doc's side, George touched the man's shoulder and whispered, "I'll keep my promise and do whatever it takes. You didn't die for nothing. I will deliver the medicine."

He closed his eyes a moment and then stood. That's when he realized the case had disappeared, and with it the cure for Jonathan and his parents.

George frowned. Who'd steal medicine from a dying man?

It had to be the same person who'd laid out Doc in the sand.

16

___

MIDNIGHT BAKERY

"You have a death wish?" the farmer asked. "What's so important about a brown bag? Is it full of money?"

"No," George said, afraid if he told the man it was medicine for Kalaupapa, the man would react like Claire's father and refuse to help. "But it's important. I have to get it back. I promised Doc."

"I'm not going near that crazy white kahuna's place. I'll drop you off the end of his road and you can hike in."

___

George felt like a real spy, crouched on the grassy knoll overlooking Larry Lee's place.

The shack was a lot like its owner—a mess with its faded paint, broken windows, and garbage piled everywhere.

The wind shifted and George caught a whiff of something foul. Worse than rotting fish on the beach or the sugar mill on a windless day. A smell something like Larry Lee himself, but intensified.

George would have to tough it out. He'd breathe through his

mouth, reclaim the case, and get out of there in less time than it took to crack a coconut.

Staying low, George made his way around to the back of the shack and crept down to the north wall. He pressed his ear to the rough wood and listened. Inside, it sounded like a chainsaw hummed.

George eased over to a broken widow and peered in. It was one big room inside. Larry Lee lay on a filthy cot, face down with his head hanging over the edge. His ropey hair spilled down to the floor. The chainsaw noise was Larry Lee snoring.

Around him were piles. Boxes. Wire. Old clothes. Hubcaps. Palm fronds. Parts of old bicycles and at least a dozen tires. Broken toasters. Kitchen utensils. Empty beer cans. Lots of empty beer cans.

Where was the little suitcase? The one with the medicine. And then George saw it. The small brown case poked out from under the cot, right next to Larry Lee's head. Several empty pill bottles were scattered across the hard-packed dirt floor.

Had Larry Lee swallowed the pills? Was that why he was sleeping?

George picked up a rock and tossed it into the room.

Larry Lee didn't move. He continued to snore like a broken washing machine.

George stood there for a little longer, trying to figure out how he could get the bag away from Larry Lee. He lobbed another rock. This one hit Larry Lee in the foot. Larry Lee didn't move. It was like he was dead, except for the snores.

This was great! What luck. He could sneak in, grab the bag, and get out before Larry Lee woke. It was a perfect plan.

George headed for the door. Red squawked when she saw George, hopped off the pickup, and came running. She was just like other chickens, always looking for a handout. George didn't have anything, so he picked a handful of grass and tossed it in the air. It landed and Red attacked it, pecking and scratching.

George opened the screen door and waited. When Larry Lee

didn't move, George stepped into the room and tiptoed to the end of the bed.

Getting down on his hands and feet, he crawled in slow motion and picked up the scattered medicine bottles that still had pills. One by one, he slid them into his pockets. He lay flat on the floor and reached for the handle of the case.

Larry Lee stopped snoring.

George froze.

Larry Lee rolled onto his back and grunted. "I knew you'd come, Coconut Boy," he said and sat up. "I've been waiting."

George jumped into a crouch, grabbed the suitcase, and bolted for the door.

Larry Lee was fast for an old guy. He lunged off the bed and caught George by the shirt. Holding the bag with two hands, George swung it as hard as he could and slammed it into Larry Lee's face.

Larry Lee staggered and released the shirt, giving George enough time to push through the screen door. It swung back to hit Larry Lee. The man roared and shoved it out of his way, tearing the flimsy door off its hinges.

The door fell, clipping George in the back and slicing down his right calf. He stumbled and fell.

"You can't escape!" Larry Lee shouted.

George threw the door at him.

"How dare you? I am the mighty Kahuna."

George grabbed the suitcase, scrambled to his feet, and started running. He glanced back.

Larry Lee had picked up a piece of pipe and balanced it like a spear in his left hand. His hand went back. He laughed like a wild man.

George zig-zagged through the garbage piles.

Red flew up, looking for a perch on Larry Lee's shoulder. Larry Lee lost his aim and the pipe fell short.

George jumped into the pickup, saw the key still in the ignition. He'd only driven once before, but he'd been a passenger a thousand times. He put his left foot on the clutch, his right foot on the gas pedal, and turned the key.

The pickup made an rrrrr noise and died. Rrrrrrrr. Nothing.

Larry Lee was getting closer.

George locked the doors. He stomped on the gas. The pickup roared to life. He let out the clutch too fast. The pickup jerked forward, traveled three feet, and died. That's when he saw his father's carved turtle necklace swaying next to the mongoose skull hanging from the rearview mirror. In it, he saw Larry Lee just standing there, holding Red and stroking the hen's feathers.

Larry Lee roared and let out a wild laugh, picked up the pipe, charged at the pickup, and smashed the driver's window. Glass shards peppered George's face and arm. Somehow, he managed to get the pickup in gear and took off. He looked back over his shoulder.

Larry Lee ran after him, screaming, "Watch out for the Night Marchers. They'll be watching for you."

George left him in the dust.

It was about seven o'clock and already getting dark when he reached the main road. He flipped on the lights, turned right, and headed west.

It was like he owned the road. He only passed two cars going in the opposite direction.

Five miles down the road, he decided he was far enough away to try and shift into second gear. The pickup bucked. Its gears ground in protest. The truck rolled to a stop and died. He tried to restart the engine, but had no luck. No wonder, the gas gauge read empty.

"Great!" George muttered and pounded the dash with a fist. He squinted at a road sign barely visible in the headlights' beam. Kaunakakai town limits.

He removed his father's necklace from the rearview mirror and slipped it over his neck before he grabbed the brown bag and started walking.

The night air was scented with the tantalizing aroma of fresh bread. It drew George down the darkened street like a Pied Piper to the only building with lights on. Kanemitsu's Bakery and Restaurant.

The side door was open.

George couldn't stop himself. He stepped inside. It was hot from the ovens, but all he noticed was the bread. Fresh bread rested on every flat surface and filled racks; mouth-watering bread. His stomach rumbled.

"What can I get for you, boy?" a man's voice asked. "Donuts are two cents a piece. Three dinner rolls a nickel. Both are cheaper by the dozen."

George stared at the baker and gave the man a half smile. "I don't have any money. I just couldn't resist the smell. I'll go now."

George turned to leave.

"Wait," the man said. "Help me clean up and I'll pay you in bread."

George smiled. "Thanks, Mister."

"Thomas," the man said and reached out his hand.

"Where do you want me to start?" George asked.

"Why don't you eat first? I have one last batch to pull from the oven." Thomas motioned to the cooling baked goods. "Help yourself. There's milk in the refrigerator."

George grabbed a roll and ate greedily. It melted in his mouth. Warm and soft like Tutu's homemade ones. He had another. And another.

"Try a donut," Thomas said as he set a tray of hot bread on the table. He picked up a pastry brush and painted the golden tops of the bread with melted butter. He smiled at George as he worked.

"Thanks. These are really good."

"You're not from around here?"

George, his mouth full, shook his head.

"What brings you to Kaunakakai in the middle of the night?"

George, tired of lying said, "I'm headed to Kalaupapa. My parents live there."

Thomas surprised George. He didn't say anything about lepers or leprosy. Instead he handed George a broom.

"Start out front in the cafe."

By the time George had the front area swept, Thomas had stowed the bread on racks and draped them in cheesecloth. The pastries went into the glass case in the cafe. It took only another twenty minutes and the kitchen was spotless.

"It's time to lock up," Thomas said. "You can stay here for the night."

"No, I need to go."

Thomas handed George a bag of fresh bread. "Are you sure you want to go to Kalaupapa? You could stay and work for me. I couldn't pay you, but you'd have a place to stay and all the bread you can eat."

"Thanks, but I have to find my parents."

"They won't let you stay in Kalaupapa."

George shrugged. "I'll cross that bridge when I get to it."

"Then let me give you a ride. I'll run you up to the trailhead."

George climbed into Thomas's shiny dark green Studebaker that was nothing like Larry Lee's truck.

They drove twenty minutes before Thomas pulled to the side of the road.

"You're sure you don't want to change your mind?"

"No," George said. "And thanks."

"Be careful," Thomas said. "The trail is treacherous. I know you want to get there as soon as possible, but you'd better wait until it's light. It's only three hours until daybreak. Good luck. I hope you're not afraid of heights and that you find what you're looking for."

George got out of the car.

"Thanks again for the ride."

Thomas drove away.

George peered into the night. Hopeful, yet afraid of what he'd find in Kalaupapa. So much had been hidden from him. So much he still didn't understand. Would his parents be happy to see him? Or would they turn their backs on him? He slid his hand into his pocket and rubbed Jonathan's lucky coin. At least Jonathan would be happy to see him.

He crossed his fingers and found himself wishing he wasn't alone.

17

PALI TRAIL

The sweet scent of guavas filled the night air. George stepped on something soft. It squished underfoot and oozed with a sweet fragrance.

He dropped to his knee and felt for more fruit. He wiped one on his shirt and gobbled it down. Guavas were his favorite. He gathered four more and sat against a tree. How many could he eat without getting sick?

Should he have one more, or . . .

Something moved in the bushes. Something big.

He shot to his feet and stood perfectly still.

A snort followed by lip smacking. The creature rummaged closer.

An unpleasant odor like Larry Lee drifted on the breeze. Had the man followed him? No, that was impossible. It had to be something else. What?

George grabbed a stick and held it tight. He was tired of running. Tired of hiding.

"Who's there?" he called out, throwing caution to the wind. "Come out. Show yourself."

There was more rustling. Branches snapped as something moved toward George.

"Hey!" George shouted. He jumped up and waved the stick as a huge dark shadow rushed him. George swung and felt the stick shudder as it connected. A squeal pierced the night, and the creature bolted into a patch of silvery moonlight. It was wild pig. It stopped and turned back, breathing hard.

George swung the stick again. This time it whistled in the air.

"Go away! Get out of here!"

Keeping his eyes on the creature, he squatted and felt for a rock with his free hand. A baseball-sized chunk rested by his foot. He grabbed it and flung it hard. The rock bounced off the pig's snout.

The pig turned and ran, snapping brush as it escaped.

George slumped against a tree and laughed. Overhead, stars twinkled through the leafy tree tops. He whispered, "Star light, star bright, the first star I saw tonight, wish I may, wish I might, have the wish I wish tonight. . . let me find my parents. Soon."

Exhaustion claimed him and he slept.

The blast of a car horn woke him, followed by the slam of a door. It took him a moment to remember where he was and how he'd gotten there. The sun was already in the sky. What time was it? How long had he slept?

Then came a series of thumps and bumps. George moved into the brush and crept toward the source of the sound. He watched a man unload four large canvas sacks from a car and stack them on the edge of the road. When he finished, he beeped his horn two times and drove off. What was in the oversized bags? George was about to investigate when he heard someone coming. He moved back and watched.

A man riding a dark brown mule and leading a lighter-colored mule appeared on the trail. He looked like a cowboy dressed in jeans, boots, and a large-brimmed hat. The hat made it impossible for George to get a good look at the man's face.

"Whoa, Lightning. Looks like we have a light load today."

The man slung a foot over the saddle and dismounted. He lifted the bags one by one and tied them onto the second mule. Stamped on the final bag were the words "U.S. Postal Service" in big black letters.

Finished, he remounted and headed back the way he'd come. Just as he passed George's hiding place, the mule stopped and took a bite of grass. The man removed his hat and wiped his face with a red handkerchief. George gulped. Covering the man's right cheek were huge white bumps that distorted an otherwise handsome face. That's when he noticed the hand holding the reins had only three fingers. The thumb and pinky were gone.

"Come on, Lightning. Don't have all day," the man said as he nudged the mule with two gentle kicks. The mule ambled forward. The man started to whistle a familiar tune by the Ink Spots, *To Each His Own.*

George gave the man a head start and waited until the mules were no longer visible before he started. The track was well worn and easy to follow.

Why had Thomas warned him the trail was treacherous? Except for the manure piles, it was easy walking. The flat path emerged from the canopy of trees onto a grassy trail, sunken low in the ground from centuries of travel. He slowed, putting more space between him and the mules.

Up ahead a fence had a huge sign nailed to it. George could read the bold black letters before he was even close.

RESTRICTED

NO ENTRY PERMITTED

WITHOUT PRIOR APPROVAL
PERMISSION TO ENTER MAY BE OBTAINED FROM THE
STATE DEOPARTMENT OF HEALTH
DIV. OF COMM. DISEASE.

The mules moseyed past the sign and went through an open space in the fence. The cowboy stopped and wired the gate shut before moving on. George squatted down to wait for the mules to move out of sight. He plucked a piece of grass, and in that instant the mules vanished. What? They were there. Then they were gone; poof, like magic.

George scrambled over the fence. The faint strains of whistling drifted from below his horizon. He rushed forward and stopped.

His stomach lurched.

In front of him, the world dropped off. More than three thousand feet below, the breaking surf looked like tiny white streaks. A stiff breeze assaulted his face and the low stunted growth clinging to the steep volcanic cliff. For the first time in his life, he understood the fear of heights. He crouched low, putting his hand to the ground to steady himself.

In the distance, the low trees and brush looked like velvety moss hugging the massive cliffs that plunged to the waiting sea.

George started down the trail, so steep that every step jolted his joints.

The trail narrowed to about three feet wide. In places, the cliff fell away. He wouldn't want to slip. The drop went on forever.

It had rained that morning and the trail was wet and slippery. Mud clung to his feet, and with every step Doc's bag grew heavier. Sweat stung his eyes, and he wiped his brow with the back of his hand.

The trail switched back on itself, again and again. Four switchbacks below, the mule rider's shirt looked like a mosaic picture. The branches and leaves were the grout.

Maybe because George's eyes were trained on the trail. Or maybe because the trail now ran under a canopy of lush vegetation. He forgot the cliff and the mule rider who was out of sight.

Small red fruit grew overhead, strawberry guavas. He plucked a few and ate them. They were sweet and tangy. He remembered Tutu telling him that too many would put you on the toilet for a long time.

He moved on.

Another ten switchbacks.

Halfway down, he caught his first glimpse of Kalaupapa. Near a crescent-shaped white sand beach, the tiny village was tucked in the crook of a small peninsula that jutted into the sea. A lighthouse perched at its tip.

Thomas had said the trail was only three miles long, but it seemed like it went on forever.

He counted switchback number twenty-six before the descent became less steep. He moved faster as the trail flattened and ran along the beautiful white sand beach he'd spotted from above.

Coconut palm trees swayed in the breeze.

Plop.

A coconut hit the ground behind him and bounced off the trail.

George smiled. He was ready for a drink of coconut milk.

George grabbed it and looked for a place to hide. He was so close to his destination. He didn't want to get caught now.

He found a sharp piece of lava and set to work removing the nut's husk. It was hard not having the proper tools. At last he was successful. He smashed the end of the coconut and managed to save at least half of the milk. He drank it greedily.

Then he broke the coconut into five chunks and gnawed on the sweet meat.

Rested, he got back on the trail. Around one turn he startled three deer, two does and a buck. They bolted up the mountain and disappeared.

George halted when the trail opened onto a large grassy field. On the far side he could see a cluster of buildings.

He couldn't risk walking across the field. He'd be seen. So he moved off the trail and stayed in the trees, making a semicircle through the brush and walking four times as far to reach the settlement.

The homes looked like any other small community. Some houses were ramshackle, needing paint like Larry Lee's. Other houses were painted and had mowed lawns with flowers like a park.

On the way down the trail he'd come up with a plan. First he'd find Jonathan. Then Jonathan would help him find his parents. But there were people everywhere, going about their business. How would George ever find Jonathan? He couldn't just walk into a store and ask if anyone knew his friend.

He squatted and watched from a distance. He'd need a better plan. Not just any plan, but a great one. Okay, he thought, as soon as it got dark, he'd sneak in. It'd be easier to hide and once everyone was off the streets he'd explore.

An orange cat appeared. It sat and ignored George as it began washing its paws.

"Hey, Kitty," he said and reached out to pet it.

The cat hissed and struck George's hand, clawing him.

George jumped up, forgetting that he'd been hiding.

"Hey!" a man shouted. He was standing by an old Oldsmobile with its hood up.

George froze.

18

THE VIRGINIAN

George dropped to his knees, clutching Doc's bag. He held his breath and waited, hoping he was invisible behind the bush.

"Over here, Ralph," the man shouted. "Did you find a distributor?"

"No, they'll have to order one from topside," a second man yelled back.

George breathed a sigh of relief. The man hadn't seen him.

The car hood slammed. "Then help me push this junk heap out of the way. It can stay here until the part comes in."

George waited until the men left. He had to find somewhere to conceal himself until it got dark. A hiding place where he could watch what was happening in town and maybe, if he was lucky, he'd spot Jonathan. Then he saw the perfect place. An abandoned house surrounded by tall grass.

It was obvious no one had lived there for a long time. The windows were broken. The front porch sagged and there were only faint traces of paint on its weathered exterior. Someone a long time ago had planted a shade tree with large, broad leaves. It had grown huge and its branches poked through a hole in the front wall and out another hole in the roof. The house should be a safe place to hide. No one in their right mind would risk entering the place.

George moved closer and crept into the yard. Up close, the house looked like it was about to collapse in on itself. He tossed the bag inside and then put his weight on a window sill. The wood creaked and tore away in his hands as he scrambled. He dropped down and leaned against the wall, breathing hard.

In the next room a man's voice asked, "You hear that? What was it?"

"Who knows," a second man said. "Hand me that hammer. The sooner we finish tearing down this place, the better."

George grabbed the bag and vaulted back through the window. He crouched lower. What was he going to do now? He stared up into the branches of the tree and smiled. It would make a better hiding place.

He climbed high into the cover of the broad flat leaves. Unless someone stood under the tree and looked straight up, they'd never spot him. He threaded the bag's handle onto a short, sturdy branch. Once he was sure it was secure, he straddled a strong limb, leaned against the trunk, and settled back to wait.

The men worked all afternoon, salvaging wood from the old house. George never saw them, but he heard pounding and heard them tromping in and out the back door. Not once did they come into front yard and because of the noise they made, George only caught snatches of their conversation.

"Wonder what Jack brought down for tonight?" the first man said.

"Don't know, haven't heard."

"Miss Hattie isn't too happy. The wild pigs have been in her trash four times this week."

"Sounds like it's time for a luau," the second man said.

The men finally left. George wiggled his toes. He tried to shift his position and stretch. It felt like the tree had made permanent dents in his skin, and his back was numb.

A bell tolled.

Two more hours and still no sign of Jonathan or anyone who remotely looked like it could be his father or mother. Of course, it was hard to get a good look at anyone. They all seemed to wear hats.

He was thankful when the sun finally slipped behind the hills. He was about to climb down when two women strolled past, their voices clear in the still night.

"What's the name of the movie, again?" one asked.

"*The Virginian*. And it's in Technicolor."

A movie!

They had movie theater here. That's exactly the place to find Jonathan.

George tossed the leather bag into the grass and slid down the trunk. It felt good to be on the ground. He stretched his stiff muscles, feeling suddenly energized.

He jogged after the two women, slowing to a walk when he caught sight of them again.

They joined a crowd going into a large building. It had to be the biggest building in town. George waited until the last of the stragglers entered. Five minutes later, the lights went out. The windows went black for a moment and then faint flickering lights danced on the windowsills. George moved to a side window and peeked inside.

He tried to search the faces in the audience, but it was too dark. There were too many people, at least three hundred or more. He found his attention drawn to the movie screen.

It was in color! He'd never seen a color film before, but there it was, the Wild West in living color. On the screen a bunch of brown and white cattle were blocking the railroad tracks. Some people on the train were mad at the delay. The cowboys didn't care. They had cows to herd.

The bad guy pulled his gun. He was easy to spot, dressed in black from the tip of his boots to the top of his cowboy hat.

"Watch out," George whispered and clamped his hand over his mouth. If he wasn't careful, someone might notice him. But maybe not. Everyone was focused on the screen. Still, it'd be smarter to stand back from the window so no one could see him from inside.

The black-mustached villain pointed his gun at a cowboy in a white hat. The hero, thought George. Too bad it wasn't that easy to spot the good guys and bad guys in real life.

When the film ended, George sprinted away from the window. The lights came on, splashing square patches of light on the grass. He looked for a place to hide near the door so he could spot Jonathan when he came out.

George ducked behind a bush. A side door opened, and a stream of nurses, nuns, and doctors came out. It was obvious they weren't patients from the way they dressed. Two minutes later, the front door opened and the real patients streamed out.

Everyone was talking.

The doctors and nurses went one way, the patients another.

The light over the front door was weak. It was hard to get a good look at anyone as they hurried down the steps. Flashlights blinked on. Small groups headed off in different directions.

A boy paused on the steps. Was that Jonathan? It kind of looked like him.

George whistled their secret code.

The boy moved down the steps and walked away.

No, it wasn't him.

Then George saw him. There was no mistaking the cock of Jonathan's head or the roll of his shoulders. This was his best friend, his blood brother. It was Jonathan. He looked the same, except that his right eyelid drooped, giving him a sleepy-eyed look a little like Humphrey Bogart.

George whistled.

Jonathan halted on the steps and looked puzzled. He bit his lip, then shook his head as if to shake off a bug and stepped onto the path.

George whistled louder and longer.

Jonathan stopped again, tilted his head. Blinking hard, he stared into the darkness.

George continued to chirp, going lower as Jonathan moved closer.

Jonathan blew a weak albatross call.

George leaped from the shadows and, using his best Bela Lugosi voice, said, "I've come to drink your blood."

"George?" Jonathan said. "Is it really you?"

"You don't think I'm the invisible man, do you?"

Jonathan's good eye opened wide and a grin spread on his face. "Shhh," he warned and motioned for George to follow. Once they were out of earshot, he said, "I can't believe it's you. That you're here."

George pulled the Chinese coin from his pocket flipped it to Jonathan. "You forgot this, so I had to bring it to you."

Jonathan caught the coin and rubbed it between his fingers. "I can't believe you're here."

George pounded Jonathan on the back.

Jonathan started coughing. When he stopped, the grin had left his face. He sounded almost angry. "You can't stay."

"I have no place to go," George said. "Kapuna and Tutu were caught in a storm. They're gone. Mr. Kim tried to have me arrested."

Jonathan frowned. "It isn't safe. You'll get the disease. You don't want to end up like me."

George studied his friend's face. "You look fine. The same as you did before, except your right eye kind of droops. It makes you look like a movie star. You don't look like the other lep. . ."

"Go ahead and say it," Jonathan said. "Leper. That's what I am. And I'm not the same. Look at my arms and chest."

He pulled up his shirt. Even in the moonlight George could see that white skin patches and sores covered Jonathan's chest like he'd been splattered with bleach.

"It's getting worse. You've seen the others. Soon I'll look like them."

George shook his head. "No, you won't. I have the medicine that will cure you." He held up Doc's suitcase.

"Stop it, George. This isn't pretend. It's real." Jonathan laughed bitterly. "Your make-believe pills won't cure me. Do you know how many people have died since I got here? Two or three a week. Someone died today. I heard the bell."

George set the bag on the ground and opened it. He took out a bottle. "This medicine will cure you. And once it does, you and I will leave this place."

Jonathan shook his head, "I'll never leave."

George grabbed Jonathan's arm and gently twisted it. "Listen! This is the cure. I met a man from Louisiana. He said the medicine was for the patients at Kalaupapa. He was a doctor that worked in a leprosarium. He said the pills kill the bacteria that causes the disease. Just try it."

George released Jonathan's arm, opened a bottle, and spilled two pills into the palm of his hand. "Take them."

Jonathan swore, grabbed the pills and tossed them in his mouth. He gagged as he dry swallowed them. "Okay, George. I took your lousy pills. You happy?" His next words came out in a whisper. "I'm still going to die."

"We all die. But you're not going to die from leprosy."

"Yeah, right."

"Doc said it will take a few days to kill the bacteria, so you have to take all the pills in this bottle. Promise you'll take them or I'll shove them down your throat."

He pushed the bottle into Jonathan's hand

"Okay, I promise. Now just leave. Go find your parents. This island is small. It shouldn't be too hard to find them."

George pulled the crumpled envelope from his pocket. "That's why I'm here. They live in Kalaupapa, and I need your help to find them."

19

NIGHT SHELTER

"**Y**ou'll have to go alone," Jonathan told George. "It's the only safe place I can think of for tonight. Father Damien's spirit will watch over you."

"What?" George said. "Have you got religion?"

"No one survives in Kalaupapa without God."

George didn't comment. He passed Doc's bag to his other hand and to change the subject asked, "Where should I meet you tomorrow? Should I come back here?"

Jonathan shook his head. "No, I'll come to you. Don't expect me too early in the day. I have school, and I need time to see if I can find news of your parents. Here, take my flashlight."

"I don't need it. The moon's bright."

"Then let me walk you to Damien Road. From there it's only a four-mile walk to Kalawao. It's where the first leper colony was put, and Father Damien's church is still there."

"I don't want to go to church," George said. "I'm here to find my parents."

Jonathan ignored the comment. "St. Philomena should be deserted this time of night." Jonathan chuckled. "Unless you run into some night zombies and they invite you to a meat and eat party. Get it? You'd be the meat for them to eat."

George groaned, but he was laughing at the same time. "Now you sound like the Jonathan I know. Even if that was a pitiful attempt at humor."

A dog barked in the distance and was answered by one closer at hand. They'd come to the edge of town.

"You're on your own from here," Jonathan said. "See ya tomorrow."

"Tomorrow. And don't forget to take the pills."

"Yes, sir!" Jonathan saluted, executed a sharp military turn and marched off.

George watched until his friend's silhouette blended into the shadows. In the distance the Molokai lighthouse sent its beam of light into the night.

George started his lonely trek to the other side of the peninsula. Cats mewed from the bushes and he felt their glowing eyes watch him as he passed. He briefly wondered if they hunted in packs like wolves, stalking their victims before they attacked. He turned and lunged, making a loud hissing sound of his own. They scattered.

An abandoned Model T Ford had been pushed to the side of the dirt road. It'd been there for enough years for a tree to burst though its hood and grow twenty feet into the sky. Further on, a row of evenly spaced pillars loomed like shadow sentinels on watch. George hurried on.

A coconut lay in the road. Laughing, George jogged toward the nut, Doc's case bumping his leg as he ran. He kicked the coconut like it was a soccer ball. It bounced and came to a halt near a stone wall lining this section of the road.

George aimed his third kick at a break in the stone wall.

"Yes!" he shouted. "It's a field goal! George Kahula wins the game!" He raced down the road, running with newfound energy.

He emerged from the trees and saw the dark silhouette of a

church. The sound of waves beat the shore close by. This had to be St. Philomena.

He hadn't slept inside a building in a long time. Not since he'd left home. It seemed like a lifetime ago.

He opened the front door and waited for his eyes to adjust. The room was dark except for beams of moonlight streaming through the windows. Patches of light littered the pews and floor.

George stepped in and let the door slide shut behind him. Inside, it was silent except for faint murmurings.

George felt his heart leap into his throat. He wasn't alone. A faint voice whispered, "Hail Mary, Mother of Grace, hear my prayer."

It was a woman's voice.

George stepped back and felt for the door with his free hand. He squinted and made out the outline of a dark shadow. It was a nun, kneeling at the front.

George pushed the door open and fled.

He ran across a large field. Overhead in the moonlight a flock of birds circled high in the night sky. Birds should not be out at night, he thought, and ran harder. Dark clouds swirled to block the moon, and the birds disappeared. Below, the surf pounded and he caught a fleeting glimpse of the rocky shoreline before the sky darkened and let loose a hard, torrential rain.

George ducked into a recess in the hill and realized it was a cave entrance.

He wished he had taken Jonathan's flashlight. Using the leather bag for balance, he crab walked into the cave.

Then using the suitcase as a cushion, he sat on it. Slumped forward, head in hands and elbows on knees, he tried to sleep. He closed his eyes, but sleep wouldn't come. He'd come so far, but somehow felt empty. The excitement of arriving and seeing Jonathan had faded. Now he felt afraid. What if his parents didn't want to see him? He wished he hadn't come. What would he do? Then he remembered Quidilla saying life wasn't fair. It was what you made it. He sighed.

How long till daybreak?

George heard something near the cave entrance. His eyes snapped open. Every muscle tensed. It sounded like something greedily gulping in air. He thought of the pig topside. Was this a bigger one, or something worse? Whatever it was, it blocked the cave's exit.

George shifted into a runner's crouch, clutching the bag like an overlarge football. He readied himself to bowl down the creature. Why had he been so stupid? Trapping himself so that now he was some creature's prisoner or its prey. In his exhaustion, he thought it might even be the night zombies Jonathan had joked about.

A shower of lava pebbles clattered from the cave entrance.

"Who's there?" a voice called.

George didn't answer.

"This is my place. You have no right to be here." The voice was young, angry, and male.

"I know you're in here. Speak up!" The words bounced off the cave walls.

George's arms tightened on the case and he tried to sound like Kapuna when he coaxed a dog. "I'm here waiting out the rain," George said.

"Get out."

"Just let me stay until it stops raining. Okay?"

"Who are you?" the belligerent voice demanded. "I don't recognize your voice."

"A traveler."

The voice snorted and gave a bitter laugh. "No one travels to Kalaupapa. You must be a new patient. Don't you like your new accommodations? Don't think you can run away from here."

"I'm not running away," George said. "I've been running toward here for a long while."

"Give me your name."

"George. And yours?"

"Masaka. My dog is Chloe."

George heard Masaka move farther into the cave. Squinting,

George could make out the man's shadow in the gloom, but not his features.

Masaka bent and set something down. A little dog danced across the lava floor, yipping at George.

"She won't hurt you. Her bark is worse than her bite."

The little dog jumped on his legs.

"She likes you," Masaka said. "That's good enough for me. You can stay until morning, and then you need to find your own cave."

"Thanks."

The little dog danced around George, jumping on his legs and bouncing like a wind up toy,

"You can hold her if you want."

George put down the case and sat on it again. The little dog jumped into his lap and tried to climb his chest to lick his face. It tickled.

"She's a hairless Chinese poodle. I brought her with me."

"How long have you been here?"

Masaka sat before he answered. "They caught me at school, I was thirteen. They didn't even let me say goodbye to my family. I was taken to the Kalaheo Receiving Station in Honolulu. The Board of Health didn't waste any time. In less than a week I was transported." He paused. "They sent me here to die, that's what they told me."

"How many years ago?"

"Ten. At first I was scared and alone, but it got better. I didn't die."

"It must have been hard."

"My girlfriend married someone else."

"I don't have a girlfriend," George said and thought about Claire.

"The days were easier. There was school. Visits to the doctor, but at night it really stinks. That's when you're alone with yourself and you remember what you've lost."

"Don't you have friends here?" George asked.

"I did. Many died, and those who didn't, turned on me after Pearl Harbor was bombed. They called me a Jap and worse, like it was my fault." He laughed bitterly. "I've never been to Japan. I was born here in Hawaii. So were my parents and grandparents, and yet I was found guilty and shunned even in this place of living hell. Didn't do nothing wrong and am treated like a criminal."

George moved off the suitcase. "I can help you. I have medicine."

Masaka laughed. "There's no help for me. I'd be better off dead, but I can't leave Chloe alone. Do you know how many miracle cures they've tried? Most of them worse than this damned disease."

George opened Doc's bag and removed a bottle. "This is different. I got it from a doctor who was bringing it here when he was shipwrecked. He swore it worked. Take it for a week and you'll see."

"I guess it can't hurt." Masaka reached for the bottle.

Their hands met and George realized Masaka had no fingers. He took the tiny bottle between his palms and tried to open it, but couldn't. He handed it back.

"You'll have to open it for me."

"One more thing. Doc said the pills won't change you back to how you were before. It can't grow back your fingers or improve your eyesight, but it'll heal your sores and you won't get any worse."

They talked until the pale light of morning filtered through the cave opening and George got his first look at Masaka.

"So how do I look? You still want to be my friend?"

The young man's face was expressionless. The leprosy had paralyzed the muscles, and he had tumor knots all over his face. His skin was spotted and he wore thick glasses that magnified his watery eyes.

"You're still you," George said.

"Why did you come here?"

"To bring the medicine. And to find my parents."

"They won't let you stay."

"That's what Jonathan says, but I have nowhere else to go."

"Who's Jonathan?"

George told Masaka his story. When he finished, they sat in silence.

"Masaka?" a lilting woman's voice sang into the cave. "I've come with your weekly supplies."

"Hide!" Masaka hissed. "It's Sister Mary Martha. She's kind, but you don't want her to find you here. Not if you want to see your parents."

20

KAUHAKO POND

George lay on his back, stretched out on the soft grass in the shade of a low lava wall. He heard Jonathan's whistle and sat up. Jonathan rode a black spotted horse. George returned the whistle and waved.

Jonathan spotted George, kicked the animal's flanks like a real cowboy, and trotted over. He dismounted and let the horse munch on the grass.

"What are you doing?" Jonathan asked, sounding a bit annoyed.

"Just waiting. You took long enough."

"Get up. You're sitting on a grave."

"Spooky," George said.

"It's not funny. Do you know how many people are buried here?"

George shrugged and pointed to a small graveyard next to the St. Philomena Church. "I thought that was the graveyard. Your Father Damien is buried there."

"No he's not."

"Is too," George argued. "I read the headstone. It's Father Damien's grave."

"Was his grave," Jonathan said. "They took his body back to Belgium."

"Why?"

"Because they wanted to honor him for his work he did here."

"Okay," George said, sounding skeptical. "That makes absolutely no sense. If he chose to live and die here, shouldn't his body still be here? Or at least . . ."

"Your fingers and toes don't fall off when you have leprosy."

"That isn't what I was going to say."

"But that's what you were thinking, isn't it."

"No it isn't, but now that you mention it, a lot of people seem to be missing them."

"I can't believe how immature you are," Jonathan said.

"Well, I can't believe how stuffy you've become..."

"If you feel that way, feel free to leave." Jonathan swung himself into the saddle. He urged the horse forward.

George walked alongside. "Come on, you know I was just kidding. What did you find out about my parents?"

"Nothing yet."

"Why not? You've had the whole morning."

"It's a little harder than you think. I was in class. I couldn't ask the nuns or they'd get suspicious. And I couldn't ask the other kids because they wouldn't know."

"Then how are you going to find out anything?"

"I have a plan."

"What?"

"I'm not telling you. You'll have to just wait and see."

"So you don't have a plan," George said. "Some things never change."

Jonathan smiled. "Trust me."

George playfully punched Jonathan's leg.

"Hey!" Jonathan said and laughed. "Race you to the crater pond." He kicked the horse's flanks. The horse went into a fast trot.

"Not fair," George shouted and ran after them.

Jonathan slowed the horse and George caught up. He jogged alongside.

"Where are you taking me? Are we almost there?"

"It's cool. You'll love it," Jonathan said and pulled the horse to a stop. "You want to ride?"

"No, I'm fine," George panted.

Jonathan jumped off, and they walked down an overgrown trail until they reached a large pond surrounded by thick jungle brush.

"This," Jonathan said with a flourish of his hand, "is the top of a volcano. The lower you dive, the warmer it gets. Who knows when it'll blow? Dare you to jump in."

George stripped to his underwear. "I double dog dare you."

Jonathan took off his shirt and George got a good look at the large splotches of white skin. And the sores. "You take the medicine I gave you?"

"Yeah, like it'll do any good."

"It will. I swear it will. Just wait. In three days you'll see results."

"Race you across the pond. Last one there is a Spam-head." Jonathan jumped in feet first. He splashed George, who was still on the shore.

George dove in like an Olympic swimmer. He matched his strokes to Jonathan's and they reached the far shore side by side.

"I guess this makes us both Spam-heads," George said, laughing.

They swam back and sat on warm rocks to dry off.

George told Jonathan about his adventures getting to Molokai. When he finished, he asked, "How's Alice?"

"She's not here."

"You mean?" He tried to find the words.

"No. It's not what you're thinking. She's lucky. They tested her and she doesn't have it. They sent her home."

"That must have made your auntie happy. At least one of you came home," George said and then wished he hadn't said it that way. It's just that he remembered how upset she'd been when he'd talked to her that night. The night he and Jonathan had become blood brothers. It seemed like it was a million years ago that they'd gotten in trouble because of trampling Mr. Kim's garden. So much had happened since then.

George changed the subject. "Tell me about your Father Damien. Who was he? Did you meet him?"

"No. I know it might seem like it, but I haven't been here that long. He died over fifty years ago."

"Oh. Where was he from?"

"Belgium." Jonathan looked at the sky. "Did you know that they used to bring the patients here on boats and throw them into the ocean? They had to swim to shore. A lot of them didn't make it. They drowned."

"You're kidding. They didn't really do that?"

"Yes, they did. It was an awful place before Father Damien arrived. He brought law and order to the settlement. Besides being a priest, he was a carpenter. He helped them build a community. He comforted and cared for the dying and organized things to make life better. Most important, he gave them the hope of eternal life, even though they didn't have long to live. I have that hope." Pause. "You can have it, too."

Now George wished he hadn't asked about Father Damien. It was like Jonathan had morphed into someone else. A preacher.

George picked up a handful of rocks and began tossing them into the pond. He threw one sideways and it skipped six times before it splashed into the water. "Check it out," he said and pitched a flat rock to Jonathan. "See if you can do it."

"Just watch me." His rock skipped seven times.

"Do you get the news here?" George asked. "I read that in Paris girls are wearing bikinis."

"What are bikinis?"

"Two-piece bathing suits. Their stomachs are bare."

"You're kidding. I bet my auntie won't let Alice have one." Jonathan raised his eyebrows. "Did you see a picture?"

"No, just read the article, but I'd like to see one." He popped his knuckles. "What's it like living here?"

Jonathan hesitated. "We see a different movie twice a week. Monday and Friday nights. Pachoal Hall has an incredible dual sound system."

"Did you see *The Mummy's Ghost*?"

"They don't show monster movies here. Poor taste."

"I guess it would be. Sorry."

"I should go back now." Jonathan jumped up. "You asked what it's like to live here? Well, it's a lot easier if you don't think about home. Or old friends."

"You don't mean that," George said. "We're blood brothers."

21

AN ACCIDENT

The afternoon dragged into a weird limbo after their swim in the Kauaka crater. Jonathan had returned to town. Two hours later, George sat on a lava ledge near St. Philomena and watched the waves.

He couldn't stop thinking about the night he and Jonathan had become blood brothers.

"We'll share in the fight against all curses, real and imagined."

"Blood brothers forever," George said.

"Brothers forever," Jonathan echoed.

"It is done," George said. "Hey, you're getting blood on your shirt."

"Shoot! My auntie will kill me." Jonathan slipped off his shirt. On his arm, a big irregular patch of white skin gleamed in the moonlight.

"Hey, your white blob has grown. It's bigger. Now it kind of looks like a ghost. Does it hurt?"

"No. Not even if I scratch it." Jonathan dug his thumbnail into the white skin. "I can't feel a thing. Auntie Mary thinks it's from the sun."

George rubbed the burn scar on his leg. The white patch seemed larger than before. He scraped it with his fingernail. In one spot the skin felt numb. He could feel the pressure of his nail, but not the sensation of it digging into the skin. Did that mean . . . Could he be sick like Jonathan?

George stood and started pacing. They couldn't send him away if he had it, but he didn't want to die. Then he thumped his head with his hand. How stupid was he? Duh . . . He had Doc's medicine. Laughing, he raced back to the cave.

"Masaka, I'm back!" George called.

The echo of his own voice greeted him.

Masaka must be somewhere else, George thought and climbed in to retrieve Doc's bag.

It was gone. Had Masaka moved it? Taken it? George frantically searched the cave.

"No," he swore and moved deeper into the cave to hunt for the precious medicine. It was darker, which made his search harder. "Please, Masaka," he whispered. "Tell me you didn't take it."

A black figure emerged from the shadows. "Is this what you're looking for?" Sister Mary Martha asked. She held up the leather bag in one hand and a bottle of medicine in the other.

"That's mine," George said.

She moved into the light. "You do not look like Doctor James H. Harrington."

"I'm not, but Doc gave that medicine to me to bring . . ." He let his voice trail off. He wasn't a Catholic, but he didn't like the idea of lying to a nun and if he said anymore, he would. "I need it."

"Do you," she said. "I don't recognize you, and I know everyone, at least by sight."

"Where's Masaka?"

"He came to me for food. When I pressed him why he was suddenly eating enough for two, he confessed that he was harboring someone from the outside. Someone who'd brought more useless medicine that was supposed to cure the *lepela*."

George swallowed. "This medicine is for my family."

"This medicine is for no one. I'm going to destroy it."

"You can't. It's not yours."

She strode out of the cave and hurried toward a small drop-off overlooking the sea. George rushed after her.

"I won't let them experiment on any more patients. They've suffered enough."

"Please. Give it to me. It's mine."

She swung the case back, as if intending to throw Doc's bag into the ocean.

"No!" He grabbed for the case. "I can't let you do it."

He caught hold and yanked on the suitcase. She wouldn't let go. The nun was strong for a woman and held on like it was a life and death tug-of-war. For George it was. The lives of his parents depended on the medicine. He couldn't let go.

She wouldn't either.

They both pulled with all their might.

George lunged forward, hoping to put her just enough off balance that she'd loosen her grip. He'd pluck the bag from her and run. There was no way she could catch him. Not in her long bulky skirts. It might have worked, but when he let go, she teetered and lost her balance.

Oh no! What had he done?

Stumbling back, she screamed, lost her footing and rolled down the embankment, taking the medicine with her. She sprawled on a rock ledge below. Waves threatened to crash over her. Doc's bag lay at her feet. If a big wave came, both it and the nun would be washed out to sea.

She looked dead. A trickle of blood seeped from a wound on her forehead.

George scrambled down, scraping his hands on the razor-sharp rocks.

She wasn't moving, but then he saw the rise and fall of her chest. She was unconscious, but alive. He scooped her into his arms and struggled to carry her up the embankment. He kept stepping on her dress and slipping. After dropping her once, he managed to get her up to the trail and laid her on the grass.

He still had to retrieve the medicine. He dashed back down the hill, falling and cutting his knees. A huge wave engulfed him and, to his horror, the leather bag washed off the rock shelf before he could get to it. It bobbed a few feet from the treacherous shoreline.

Without thinking, George jumped in.

He hardly felt the sting of the salt water on his cuts.

Another wave smashed him into the rocky lava.

George floundered for a moment and then pushed off with his feet. He got his hand on the bag and grabbed its handle.

Another wave lifted him and dashed him on the rocky ledge. The leather bag saved his face.

He scrambled to his feet. Blood streaked his skin from fresh cuts and scrapes. There was a gash on his leg just below his burn scar. He ignored the sharp pain and climbed back up the steep slope to where he'd left the nun.

Sister Mary Martha had rolled onto her back. She sat up and winced as she touched her right foot.

"It's my ankle," she said and groaned. "I think I've sprained it. Help me stand."

"Let me carry you," George said.

"Nonsense," she said. "You're hurt. I think I can walk, if you assist me."

George helped her to her feet. He put his arm under hers and half carried her to St. Philomina's.

"This isn't going to work," he said. "I have to go for help."

George deposited her on the church steps and went back for Doc's bag.

"Where are you going?" she called after him. "You're going the wrong way."

"I have to get the medicine."

"Oh," she said, rubbing her left temple with her hand.

He grabbed the bag. He couldn't let them have it unless they promised to give it to his family. There wasn't enough for more than five or six patients.

He spotted two trees twisted together to form one odd-looking trunk. It shouldn't be too hard to find it again. He rolled back a lava boulder and took the medicine bottles from the bag. He popped one open, gulped down three pills and then placed the bottles in the recess. He replaced the rock and scattered dried leaves at its base.

With the empty bag in his hand, he returned to Sister Mary Martha. She was unconscious.

"Father Damien," he whispered. "If what Jonathan says about you and your God is true, watch over the nun. Don't let her die."

Grabbing the empty bag, George raced down the road. He didn't stop until he reached Kalaupapa. He banged on the first door he came to. "A nun needs help," he shouted. No one was home. He tried a second house and a third. No one answered.

Church bells rang. Everyone must be at church, he thought. He followed the bells until he came to a tall white church with three arches over a porch. He raced up the stairs, through the center arch. He dropped the bag on the steps and burst into the church. A hundred faces turned to stare at him.

"Sister Mary Martha has fallen and needs help!" he shouted. "She's on the steps at St. Philomena."

He'd done his duty and now it was time to get out of there before he got caught. He turned and bolted back out through the double doors. He put on an inhuman burst of speed and jumped over the first three stairs. His right foot landed on Doc's bag and skidded. His arms flapped the air, trying to hold his balance.

Behind him, people streamed from the church.

He felt himself falling. The last thing he remembered was the sharp jolt of pain on the back of his head as it connected with the bottom step.

22

HOUSE ARREST

George rolled on his side and smiled. He was almost awake, but not ready to open his eyes. Not yet. The bed was soft, cozy and clean. He didn't want to leave its warm embrace. What a strange dream, he thought. I wonder what Tutu is fixing for breakfast? Hope it's Spam and rice.

"Is he awake?" an unfamiliar woman's voice asked.

He stiffened. It hadn't been a dream. He opened his eyes and winced at the bright light streaming in through the window. He wasn't back home, but in a small room with pale green walls. On one wall was a cross with a tortured Christ.

The place smelled of disinfectant, like what Tutu used to clean the toilet. A nun strode through the open door.

"He's awake now," she said to someone outside the room. To George she said, "How are you feeling?"

George struggled to sit up, and felt a sharp pain stab the back of his head. Blinking back tears, he tried to shift positions but couldn't. His leg weighed a ton, and every inch of him hurt.

"Just relax," the nun said and flipped back the bed sheet.

His right leg was in a cast.

"Where am I?" George asked. His brow wrinkled. The last thing he remembered was swimming. Racing Jonathan across a lake surrounded by jungle brush. Slowly it all came back.

He was in Kalaupapa. Searching for his parents.

"Let me assist you," the nun said and helped him into a sitting position. "You had a nasty fall, but don't worry. You're young, healthy and will heal."

She started to leave.

"Wait."

She paused at the door and turned to face him.

"Is Sister Mary Martha all right?"

She smiled and said, "She's doing much better than you."

George flopped back against the pillow. The last thing he remembered was leaving her on the steps of the church. What happened to the medicine? He remembered struggling with the nun and her falling, but what had happened to the bag after that?

Another nun, younger than the first, came in with a bowl of broth. "Drink this. It'll make you feel better."

George took the cup. "Thanks."

She left.

He sipped the lukewarm liquid, barely tasting it. What had he done with the bag? He could see it floating in the ocean and remembered jumping in after it. He'd saved it, but after that it was a blank. Sister Mary Martha must have given it to the doctors? That must be why they were treating him so nice.

"Pssst. George!"

George looked to the door.

"Over here."

George's gaze swung to the window.

It was Jonathan. "You okay?" he asked.

"Yeah, like a top. At least my head is spinning like one."

Jonathan laughed. "Only you would joke at a time like this."

"I'm not joking. Turning my head too fast makes me dizzy. What are you doing out there? Why don't you come inside so I don't have to twist my head to look at you?"

"You don't understand anything, George. This is a clean wing. Lepers aren't allowed."

"What? I thought this was a hospital."

"It is, but not for us. We have our own separate clinic. And separate bathrooms. Separate movie entrances. Separate housing."

"Why?"

"They're afraid that if they mix with us, they'll get sick. And speaking of sick, George, you're not going to believe this. I think that medicine you gave me worked. The sore on my elbow is healed. And so are the ones on my back."

"Take off your shirt. Let me see."

"My skin's still white, bit I feel great. And Masaka's sores have healed, too."

"That's great."

"I'm sorry I didn't believe you."

"Have you told anyone?"

Pause.

"No, just Masaka. I think he told them about you and the medicine, but not about me."

George grinned. "You know you really messed up when you left your lucky coin behind. It's a good thing I gave it to you and didn't keep it for myself."

Jonathan laughed. "I don't know about the coin, but my prayers were answered."

George didn't say anything. He wasn't sure how he felt about Jonathan's newfound religion. He didn't believe in Jonathan's god, or leprosy wouldn't have existed in the first place. And Kapuna and Tutu wouldn't have drowned at sea. And his parents . . .

"George?"

"Yeah."

"I have more good news. I found your parents."

"They're still here? And my sister?"

"I'm sorry, George. She died two months ago, but your parents are still alive."

George swallowed. He felt a little guilty that he was more excited about finding his parents than sad about her death. But it's not like he'd known her. She was just a name. Still . . .

Jonathan interrupted his thoughts. "You have to give them the medicine. What did you do with the rest of it?"

George tightened his lips. "I don't know. I think they have it."

"They?"

"The doctors."

Jonathan shook his head. "I don't think so. The buzz is that they were expecting a doctor from Louisiana to come with a new miracle drug, but he never arrived. Then when Masaka seemed cured, and they found out about you, everyone started talking. Everyone wants the drugs."

"I can't remember what happened to it. Even if I could, there's not enough for everyone. Just for a few people. I know it's not fair, but I want my parents to be the first to get the treatment. They can send for more medicine from Louisiana."

Footsteps sounded in the hall. George turned toward the door. "Someone's coming."

A tall, stern-looking man entered the room. George knew he was a doctor because of the stethoscope hanging over his shoulders.

The first words out of his mouth weren't words of comfort. "Where is the medicine?"

George felt like he was in the principal's office, being grilled to find out who had put glue on the teacher's chair.

"We know you had it. Sister Mary Martha told us, and we've seen the results in Masaka. Now tell me, where did you hide the drugs?"

"They're in the bag," George said. "But I'm not sure where it is. The last thing I remember was going back for it after the nun was hurt."

"This bag?" The man held up Doc's leather case. "It's empty. I don't know what kind of game you're at, but you need to quit fooling around. Tell me, what have you done with the medicine?"

"I don't know," George said. "I can't remember, but if and when I do, I want my parents to have it first."

"So that's your game. Well, it's not for you to decide."

"It will be if I can remember."

"So you're pleading amnesia? I don't buy it. It's a little too convenient. Who are you?"

"I came to find my parents. Harry and Lily Kapuna."

"Kapuna," the doctor said. "The name is familiar. They had a girl about your age. She died last month. Your father's a mechanic."

"I've come to live with them. To help them."

"That's not possible. You don't have leprosy. You don't belong here."

"I want to see them."

"That can be arranged, providing you produce the sulphone drugs."

"I would if I could," George said louder. Each word came out through clenched teeth. "I can't remember what I did with them."

"If you want to see your parents, you will remember," the doctor said in a low voice.

"It isn't fair," George shouted. "I came all this way to see them and . . ."

"Healthy children aren't allowed here," the doctor said. "As soon as you're able to travel, you must return to Maui. We'll send word to the authorities that we found you."

"What about the white patch on my leg?" George flipped the sheet back and pulled up the leg of his shorts to expose the egg-shaped patch of skin. "You can't send me away if I have leprosy."

The doctor tightened his lips into a frown. "By the grace of God, you have not contracted leprosy, in spite of your foolish and risky behavior. Thank God," the man said and pointed to George's leg. "That is a burn scar."

"Don't talk to me of God," George muttered. Angry tears of frustration threatened to spill from his eyes. "He took my parents away. He took away my best friend, He took my grandparents."

"Tell that to the patients who desperately need that medicine." The doctor shook his head and left.

What would George do now? Where could he go? Everyone he loved was dead or lived here in Kalaupapa.

"I will see my parents," George repeated.

He tried to get out of bed, but didn't have the energy to swing his legs over the side. They left him alone and the day stretched into long hours. He slept, ached and desperately tried to remember what he'd done with the medicine.

Late in the afternoon, a familiar voice greeted him.

"You look worse for wear," Sister Mary Martha said. "I want to thank you for what you did for me."

"It was my fault you were hurt."

"And I was wrong to try and destroy the medicine. It works." Pause. "George, you have to give the doctors the medicine."

George frowned. "I can't. I don't know where it is."

She smiled and shook her head. "God works in mysterious ways. You have to learn to trust Him."

"If your God is real, why is the sister I never met dead? Why does he allow good people to suffer with leprosy?"

"Perhaps it is because God wants us to deal with our life in a different way."

"That seems cruel. Why doesn't he just send a cure?"

"He did. You brought it to us." She smiled like Tutu did when she was disappointed with him. "Where did you hide the medicine?"

"I don't know," George said. "I really don't remember."

"Before I blacked out, you left me on the steps and then went back for the suitcase. Concentrate. Try to remember. So many people are counting on you. Not just your parents, but the other patients here who have suffered for so long."

She shook her head in disappointment and left.

George closed his eyes, trying to remember. "Okay, Sister Mary Martha's God, if you are real, let me remember."

And then as if he was coming out of a fog, he saw the double tree. The palm and the kukui trees twined together into one trunk. Leaves and fruit from both sprouted from the one new tree. Behind it rested a black lava boulder in the dark powdery dirt.

His eyes flew open and he smiled. "I remember!"

23

ALOHA, ALOHA

"**It's about time,**" **George complained** when Jonathan finally appeared at the window. It was dusk. "Where have you been the last two days?"

"Maybe I should come back when you're in a better mood," Jonathan said and made like he was going to leave.

"Don't go. I've remembered where I hid the medicine."

"Did you tell them?"

"No, I don't trust them."

"I talked to your dad."

"Did you tell him I was here?"

"He already knew."

"Can you bring him to me?"

"No, they're watching your room. The only reason I could come, is that I volunteered to pull weeds on the grounds. Yesterday they had me working in the front yard."

"You have to get the medicine for me."

"Then what?"

"Give two bottles to my parents. Make sure they take it. Bring the rest to me."

George told Jonathan where to find the bottles. That evening, George had the medicine and asked to speak to the doctor he'd met the first day. The one that had questioned him like he was a criminal.

"Here's the medicine," George said, pulling two bottles from under his pillow.

"What? Where's the rest of it?" the doctor sputtered. He sounded angry instead of being pleased.

"That's all that's left. It's enough for two people." George recited Doc's instructions about the dosage and results. "I've kept my end of the bargain. Now I want to see my parents."

"I'll arrange it as soon as you are ambulatory."

"Ambulatory?"

"Until you can move about by yourself."

"Why can't you bring them here?"

"Patients are not allowed in clean areas."

"Clean areas?"

"This wing of the hospital is for staff. As soon as you're able to use a pair of crutches, I'll arrange a visit. It's against the rules for children to visit, but in your case we're making an exception."

"I'm not a child," George said. "I've come a long way to see them. Bring me the crutches."

The doctor started to leave, but stopped and turned back. "We've heard from the authorities on Maui. Before the end of the week, someone will come to collect you."

It was three days before George was strong enough to navigate the hall on a pair of crutches. It was a bittersweet accomplishment. Now he'd get to meet his parents and then be banished. The superintendent had made it clear that he wouldn't allow George to return to Kalaupapa until he was sixteen. Until then, he'd be an orphan.

Midmorning the next day, Sister Mary Martha wheeled George down the ramp into the fresh air.

"You don't need to push me in a wheelchair," George complained. "I can walk on my crutches just fine."

"But I want to," she said. "You deserve a little pampering. Are you nervous?"

"A little," George admitted.

"Don't worry," she said. "They're more worried about how you'll feel about them when you see them face-to-face for the first time. Your mother is a little disfigured, but your father looks normal."

"That's not what I meant," George said. "I hope they want to see me."

"Of course they do. Visitors from outside are always welcome. Do you realize that you're the first child to visit?"

"Why is that?"

"Healthy children are not allowed here. Healthy babies are sent out to protect them. That's why you were sent to live with your grandparents."

She pushed him up another ramp and into a long room lined with windows. The room was empty except for a long table that divided the room like a low fence. Other than climbing onto the table, the only way to get to the other side was through another door.

"Let me go over the rules with you," Sister Mary Martha said. "There is to be no physical contact between you and them. You must remain on your side of the table and they on theirs. Don't exchange anything. Sit here. They'll be here in a minute," she said and left.

He closed his eyes. Let them like me, he thought.

"George?" The man's voice sounded a lot like Kapuna's, but lower in pitch.

Their eyes met. George wanted to leap over the table and hug the tall, handsome man who tottered on unsteady feet. His father.

"Dad?" George wished he had his crutches.

A second person entered.

"Mom?"

Her outline was framed in sunlight like an angel. She moved into the room. "George, my son. I can't believe it's you."

Her face under her hat was scarred and bumpy.

They sat in the two chairs provided across the table from him.

"I've come a long way to see you," George said. "Did Jonathan give you the medicine? He's my best friend."

"I knew you'd be a handsome boy," his mother said. "You were a beautiful baby. Perfect. And then they took you away." She raised a fingerless hand and wiped her eye.

"It was for the best," his dad said.

"You've grown so tall and strong like your father used to be when I fell in love with him."

George's throat tightened. He wanted to ask, *Did you miss me? Did you ever wonder how I was doing?*

It was as if his mother had read his mind. "We lived for the letters Tutu wrote about you."

There was so much he wanted to say. So much he felt, and didn't know how to express it. "How can you stand living here?"

"Because we're together," his father said. "We're luckier than most. We still have each other. And we keep busy."

"How long have you been here?"

"Your mother was diagnosed at eighteen. We'd only been married a month, and they wanted to take her from me. I couldn't let her go, couldn't live without her, so I came with her into exile."

"I didn't want him to come," she said and patted his father's hand.

"But I insisted. We were young, in love. Life wouldn't have been worth living without her by my side."

"Then you didn't have the *lepela*?"

"No, not then. I came as a *kokua*, a helper. It wasn't until after you were born that I got it."

"Knowing you were healthy and well has sustained us. We lived for the letters about you."

"I never stopped thinking about you, either." George hesitated. "I thought you didn't want me."

"You couldn't be more wrong," his father said.

"We've missed you every day," his mother whispered.

"Why couldn't you have written me? Told me the truth."

"We didn't want to burden you," she said.

"And we thought you were happy with Kapuna and Tutu."

"I was, but—"

Sister Mary Martha stepped into the room. "I'm sorry, but your time is up. People are here to take you topside, George."

"Just a few more minutes," George said. He slipped the turtle necklace from his neck and held it out across the table. "Tutu said this is yours. She said it was special. I almost lost it. I think you should have it back."

His father reached into his shirt. "No, this one is mine. Kapuna carved it for me when I was a boy. That one is yours. I carved it for you just before you were born."

George looked into his father's eyes and realized the carved turtle was, and always had been, an expression of his father's love. George slipped the necklace back over his neck, feeling a pang of regret. There was so much more he wanted to say. To ask.

"I'm sorry," Sister Mary Martha repeated. "It really is time for George to leave."

"Never forget, George, we're proud of you," his mother said.

His father stood, helped her to her feet. "Now go and lead a good life for us, and remember that wherever you go, we're with you in spirit."

"Wait!" George said. In one swift movement, he pushed to his feet, sat on the table and slung his cast on top.

"Stop!" Sister Mary Martha cried out. "You can't do that. You could get sick."

George ignored her and slid across the table. He righted himself and grabbed his mother in a fierce hug. Then he hugged his father.

A doctor ran in, and for a moment there was nothing but shouting and chaos in the room. In seconds, his parents were hustled from the room by two patients dressed as orderlies.

The visit was over.

"George." Sister Mary Martha sighed and shook her head. "Come on. It's time for you to leave."

"I don't want to go. I want to stay. I want to be a *kokua*. I don't want to go back to Maui and live with strangers."

"Don't be afraid, George. You're not in trouble. Haven't you learned that God is in control?"

George grunted, biting his lower lip to keep from crying.

"They're not angry with you. They just want to take you home."

"I want this to be my home. To stay here with my parents and Jonathan."

"Don't you want to see your grandparents? They've traveled a long way to collect you."

CHAPTER 24: GOING HOME

"Kapuna! Tutu!" George dropped his crutches and flung himself into Tutu's arms.

She hugged him fiercely.

"I thought you were dead," George said.

"And we thought we'd lost you," Kapuna said, lifting George and squeezing him.

"But your outrigger was totally smashed up. And when you didn't come home, I. . ." George's voice faltered.

"The storm took us south, but we managed to get to shore. What I didn't manage, was to pull the outrigger high enough in the sand and the sea reclaimed it." He ruffled George's hair. "But that is history. Come on, let's go home."

"Aren't you going to visit Mom and Dad?"

"We already have," Kapuna said. "This morning."

"And Jonathan," Tutu added.

"I can't go without saying good-bye to Jonathan and Masaka."

"Sorry, George, but we have to leave now," Kapuna said. "The mules need enough time to get up and back down the trail before nightfall. With your leg in a cast, it'll take longer."

Sister Mary Martha patted George on his shoulder. "Good luck and remember what I said about trusting God."

"Will you say goodbye to Jonathan and Masaka for me?" George asked.

"Jonathan asked for me to give you this." She handed George a small cross made from two square nails welded together. "He said to tell you that, he'll never be far from you and he hopes one day you'll wear it close to your heart. Until then, consider it a good luck cross."

The climb up the steep cliffs was easier on back of a mule. Still, George felt like every step the mule took jolted his mending bones. Near the top, George turned in his saddle and stared down at the peninsula far below.

"I promise I'll never forget you're here. One day I'll return."

Maybe the mule sensed its rider wanted a good look at the peninsula that jutted out below, before descending the treacherous trail. Old Jack paused at the precipice, just inches from the fifteen hundred-foot drop to the ocean below.

George gently kicked the mule's flanks, urging it forward. The animal swayed and then continued to pick its way down the steep Pali trail.

The mule tethered behind the one George rode was loaded down with presents. Bolts of bright flowered material for his mother filled one oblong box. Two square boxes held the complete set of Zane Gray novels for his father. In a fourth box, packed in thick wads of cotton batting, was a special present for Jonathan—a movie camera with twenty blank reels.

This trip, he'd only be able to stay for the summer break before he returned to his pre-med studies.

He looked down over the peninsula, remembering his first trip and the people he'd met along the way. Larry Lee, Thomas, Quidilla, the tattooed woman and the others. They'd proved one thing. No one could achieve anything on their own. Everyone needed someone. It was the relationships that kept you going. Even Mr. Kim had Poi Dog.

He felt the small box in his pocket, the final present he had to give. It would have to wait for the short visit to Halawa Valley he planned to make before he returned to school. It was a ring for Claire.

The mule turned another corner. George could see his parents' home. He nudged the mule's flanks to hurry it up. The visit would seem too short, but one day, he'd return to spend the rest of his life there. He and Claire together.

He smiled. It had been a long trip to get this far, but it was worth it.

AFTERWORD

Escape to Molokai is a work of fiction. George and Jonathan, Larry Lee, Claire, Kapuna, Tutu and the other characters in this story have been created out of my imagination about a time in recent history that was unbearable to those forced to experience the devastating effects of *Hansen's Disease*.

Before the discovery of *sulphone* drug therapy, being diagnosed with leprosy was a death sentence. Men, women, and children were arrested and sent into exile with no hope of escape. In Hawaii, more than 7,000 people died in Kalaupapa before a cure was discovered. Even for those who survived, the cure came too late to erase the damage the disease had wrought. Killing the *bacctria* that caused the disease didn't reverse the damage already sustained. I have only admiration and respect for those brave enough to have lived with those insurmountable odds.

The following is a timeline of historical events that influenced the telling of my story and is followed by a few factoids about *Hansen's Disease*.

HISTORICAL TIMELINE

1835- PRESENT

1835 -- First documented case of leprosy in Hawaii.

1863 -- Leprosy is officially recognized as a problem by the Hawaiian Board of Health.

1865 -- King Kamehameha V signs the Leprosy Act. It segregated *Lepers* and established the Kalaupapa peninsula as an isolation settlement.

1866 -- First shipment of patients arrives at Kalawao, on the peninsula.

1873 -- Father Damien arrives on the peninsula.

1889 -- Father Damien dies of leprosy.

1893 -- Hawaiian Islands becomes a United States Territory.

1898 -- Hawaii becomes an independent monarchy while at the same time remaining a United States territory.

1901 -- Lighthouse built at the tip of peninsula.

1936 -- Father Damien's remains returned to Belgium

1941 -- Pearl Harbor is bombed.

1945 -- World War II ends.

1946 -- Sulphone antibiotic therapy developed at the Carville Leprosarium in Louisiana is tried on six patients at Kalaupapa. The medication seemed to produce changes overnight.

1946 -- April 1st a destructive tidal wave strikes Hawaiian Islands - 150 people die.

1946 -- Sugar strike: 28,000 sugar workers organized into The International Longshoreman and Warehousemen's Union. More than 7,000 replacement workers were brought in to break the strike. Those from the Philippines were known as the Sakadas.

1959 --Hawaii becomes a state.

1969 -- Hawaii's isolation laws are abolished.

1974 -- The new Hawaiian penal code rescinded the laws condemning kuhunas.

1980 -- President Carter signs law establishing Kalaupapa National Park. Current patients are given life tenancy.

1980 -- The state Legislation mandates change in official terminology. The term *leprosy* is replaced by *Hansen's Disease*.

HANSEN'S DISEASE FACTOIDS

Gerhard Armauer Hansen discovered the disease was caused by a bacteria called *mycobacterium leprae*.

It affects the skin, eyes, and nerves.

The first sign is usually a discolored patch of skin. These patches can be flat or bumpy. Untreated, they develop into sores and are usually insensitive to pain from pin pricks, pressure or heat.

It affects the nerves in the hands and feet. At first there usually is a tingling or numbness before a complete loss of sensation.

When it manifests on the face, it can cause blindness.

If not treated, it gets progressively worse and usually results in permanent nerve damage and cosmetic disfigurement.

Today, a number of different antibiotics are used to treat the disease. Once treated, the patient becomes non-infectious. If treated early, there is less chance of permanent damage.

For centuries the term *leper* carried a social stigma that implied immorality and slovenliness. Because it is an infectious disease caused by a germ, not by one's moral nature or behavior, its name was changed to *Hansen's Disease*.

At the time of writing this book [2009], approximately 800,000 new cases are reported every year. Most cases are found in subtropical countries—India, Brazil, and Sub-Saharan Africa.

ACKNOWLEDGMENTS

Again I must thank my advanced readers for their support,
suggestions, editorial comments and encouragement.
Lyle Brown, Christine Sackey and Sue Wyshynski.

ALSO BY SPIKE BROWN

Saving Bigfoot Valley

Escape to Molokai

The Royal Historian of Oz

WRITING AS S. D. BROWN

The Scrapbook Riddle

The Lake Quilt Mystery

Pretty Little Rumors

I Escaped the California Camp Fire

ADULT MYSTERIES BY S.D. BROWN

Alabaster Alibi

Bloodstone Bludgeon

Calcite Corpse

Made in United States
North Haven, CT
12 April 2023

35349333R00096